Cadence looked great.

More relaxed, her smile easy and wide. Her cornflower-blue eyes sparkled as she talked with her morning regulars at the swimming pool.

Whatever happened, he'd be seeing her again regularly. But they were strangers now. There was no going back to their high school days, when they'd been practically inseparable. When he'd loved her with his whole heart. When he'd believed they were soul mates.

No such thing as soul mates, Ben told himself as he turned away from her. Failure became a tight vise in his chest until it hurt to breathe. He'd failed at every major relationship he'd ever started, and he knew he'd failed Cadence the most.

A soft lilt of laughter had him turning once again, his soul recognizing Cadence before his mind could. The instant his gaze found hers, she looked up. Their eyes met....

JILLIAN HART

makes her home in Washington State, where she has lived most of her life. When Jillian is not hard at work on her next story, she loves to read, go to lunch with her friends and spend quiet evenings with her family.

JILLIAN HART
Heaven's Touch

Steeple Hill®

Published by Steeple Hill Books™

STEEPLE HILL BOOKS

**Steeple
Hill®**

ISBN 0-373-81229-9

HEAVEN'S TOUCH

www.SteepleHill.com

Printed in U.S.A.

What is important is faith
expressing itself in love.
—*Galatians* 5:6

Chapter One

Ben McKaslin climbed out of his pickup, fished his debit card out of his wallet and hit the gas tank lever. His back complained. His leg complained.

He ignored both, because he was no longer in Florida. Gone were the stifling heat and the cloying humidity and the scents of moss and dampness and heat of the Gulf coast he'd never gotten used to. How could any place on earth be as good as Montana?

The sight of rugged amethyst peaks and green rolling meadows touched him deeply. It was good to be going home. There were lots of things he'd missed. The natural beauty of the state was one of them. He swiped at his scratchy eyes.

Well, he wasn't home yet, but ever since he'd crossed the Montana state line, he hadn't been able to drive fast enough. He hadn't wanted to stop for any reason and had kept on driving.

Except for the fact that the truck was on Empty. This stop would be a quick break to gas up and he'd be back on the road. As he glanced around the outskirts of Bozeman, he realized he was exactly fourteen minutes from the sleepy rural town where he'd grown up. Fourteen minutes from the house he'd grown up in.

He grabbed his crutches from behind the seat. The annoying sticks had gotten wedged beneath his stuffed rucksack, so he had to wrestle them out. If his leg could have supported his weight without pain, he'd have left them there, but the streaks shooting up his femur were a little too strong to ignore. Not that he was supposed to put his full weight on his leg much at all, but he fudged it a lot.

He wasn't the only one at the truck stop, and that surprised him, it being as late as it was—nearly midnight. Of course, this place was visible from the interstate, and the last pit stop for gas and food had been a good thirty miles back. He apparently wasn't the only one low on blood sugar and running out of gas.

His stomach might be growling like a bear, but he figured on waiting to raid his sister's fridge, since he knew Rachel would have stocked up for his benefit. He wouldn't want to let her down, right?

He leaned on the crutches, looking through the dark for danger. It was habit, ingrained from boot camp on through his PJ training, honed in jungles, deserts and mountains around the world. Even here in the good old U.S.A. he couldn't break the habit as he listened, senses alert, while crossing the short distance from the cab to the gas tank.

On the other side of the pump was a family vehicle, and the pleasant-looking middle-class woman in a loose pink T-shirt, cutoffs and flip-flops measured him suspiciously. She latched the lock on the handle pump, leaving the nozzle in the gas tank, and slid away from him.

It was late, it was dark, she was alone with kids—the dome light revealed two little ones fast asleep in their car seats. It showed good sense on the mother's part. Ben couldn't deny that he did look disreputable. Then again, he was paid by the government to be disreputable.

He slipped his card into the slot and waited for the screen to request his pin number, which he punched in lickety-split. His gaze swept the pump piles, which were flooded with bright light. A couple of big rigs were fueling up at the diesel pumps, designed for truckers. A late-night RV ambled in and parked on the other side of the semi's triple trailers.

The machine beeped, demanding he lift the nozzle and start pumping. He put in plain old unleaded. He was no longer a poor kid growing up in tough circumstances, but old habits died hard. He screwed off the gas cap, and as he was latching the handle lock, a small gray domestic sedan pulled up to the pump behind him.

It was a woman. When she opened her door and the dome light splashed on, he noticed her sleek dark locks of hair, thick and straight, and a heart-shaped face that could only be described as sweet. Or maybe that was his own interpretation.

Wait a minute—he knew that face. Her delicate features had matured, but it looked like...

No, it couldn't be her.

Yes, it was. He blinked his eyes, staring. It really was her. Someone he hadn't seen in person since he was a wild and woolly eighteen-year-old with an attitude and a talent for trouble.

Incredibly, Cadence Chapman emerged into the night. She was still tall and straight and slender—as graceful as a ballerina as she walked without watching where she was going. She dug through a well-worn leather wallet and withdrew a ten-dollar bill. She still had that saunter that made her look as if she were walking a few inches above the ground.

I used to love her. His heart wrenched and left him in pain, watching as she headed straight for the cashier inside the attached quick mart.

Her long dark hair fluttered behind her, midway down her back. A small brown leather purse swung from her shoulder. He wasn't in love with her anymore, but seeing her sure felt surreal, as if it was a dream or something.

He'd pinch himself, but he already knew he was awake and not dreaming. Who would have thought—Cadence Chapman? Hadn't she moved away right out of high school, with a big college scholarship and even bigger goals?

What was a world-class athlete doing in central Montana? He'd have to ask her when she came back to her car, if she recognized him.

A cell phone somewhere nearby jangled a snappy electronic tune. The woman with the kids. The tune died, and he could hear the faint murmur of her voice from the direction of the driver's seat. She must have the driver's door open, so she could listen for the pump. It gave a distinct snap, shutting off. As she spoke to someone—her husband by the sounds of it, Ben tuned her out.

The rush of gas through the pumps served as background noise as he leaned against the side of the truck bed. He had a perfect view of Cadence through the quick mart's open door. She still had that cool way about her, the one that had often annoyed him so much.

But there was something fundamentally different about her. He couldn't put his thumb on it as he watched her slip the money on the counter and exchange pleasantries with the clerk, who was a middle-aged man watching her a little too closely, as if he were getting up the nerve to flirt.

But like the old Cadence he used to know in high school, this woman didn't return the obvious interest and snapped out of the store. She had an athletic stride, and her long lean legs were tanned from the hem of her shorts all the way down to her feet. She wore practical flat sandals.

Not at all like the Cadence he remembered. That girl loved glitter, fancy shoes and designer names. She wouldn't have been caught in public wearing bargain department-store shoes.

Before he had much of a chance to wonder about that, the air changed from calm to charged, the way it did before lightning struck. He could smell danger even before the woman on the other side of the fuel pump gasped. He leaped to render aid even before the bright flash of fire hissed like a striking snake.

Time slowed as he felt the radiant blast of heat against the right side of his face. In a blink he'd crossed the meridian and was beside the woman before she could scream. This was what he was trained for, and the more the danger, the calmer he became. He was used to the kick of adrenaline that supercharged him. He didn't feel the shatter of pain in his leg or the sizzle of heat against his skin.

"Release it. Let go. Do it now."

She didn't respond. Panic was curling through her, and it was her enemy, blocking all rational thought. He caught her by the arm to keep her from flinging the hose away in panic. He couldn't let her spread the fire, over her, him or innocent bystanders.

"Drop it!" he commanded.

Only when her fingers released the handle did he shove her to the ground, rolling her on the concrete. This didn't help douse the flames greedily devouring her loose walking shorts.

Suddenly another set of hands came out of nowhere offering a dripping-wet blanket. Perfect. Just what he needed. He ignored the woman's cries of protest and smothered the flames. She was out of danger, and the identity of the person who'd come with the blanket didn't register in his thoughts as he barked commands to keep the woman back—he was already on task for the next priority.

The kids. The vehicle wasn't yet engulfed. Leaving the nozzle in the tank had bought enough time. Although he saw the first problem: the van had only one side door—on the pump side, where flames were visible through the closed window.

One toddler had started to cry. Ben dived into the driver's seat, spotted a trucker running with a fire extinguisher and barked orders. "Hit the tank, and stay back."

You've only got a few more minutes, so move, he told himself.

The air in the van was getting smoky. He twisted through the space between the seats, ignoring the awkward angle of his flexible cast. He unbuckled the crying kid, a little girl with red ringlet curls who seemed to have changed her mind about letting a stranger haul her out of her seat.

"I'll take you to your mom, okay?" he said, hauling her little wiggly form against him. Someone was there—the RV driver, he realized—so Ben shoved the girl at him.

"Go!" he shouted, choked on a mouthful of smoke. The passenger window was open and the flames were roaring.

The sleeping baby was harder to grab. He heard the squeal of a siren, the shouts from bystanders telling him to hurry and the lethal roar of the fire gaining strength. The buckle gave, the limp baby tumbled into his hands and he pulled him against his chest. The baby stirred, waking with a cry, but he was moving fast, feeling the heat and counting the seconds.

Fresh air beat across his face, and he was free. He kept on going, feeling no pain, aware only of the eerie seconds stretching out like minutes. He shielded the little one with his body, keeping on his feet as the fire surged. He felt the heat burn into his back.

The kids were safe, but he was on fire.

He hated fire.

"I'll take him." It was a middle-aged woman—probably from the RV, and he handed over the little tyke.

"Go out toward the street. Go," he told the woman and the man, who must be her husband. "No telling how dangerous this'll be if it explodes. And get everyone back."

He beat at his shirt the best he could, but he wasn't sure about where he couldn't see or reach. It couldn't be too bad, though, or he'd be in serious trouble by now. He kept smacking at the worst of it— emberlike spots mostly—and didn't give it any more thought. He had a medical situation to assess.

It wasn't as if he hadn't been on fire before. It happened to soldiers, and he was well trained.

The mom was sitting up on the ground, held back by the clerk from behind the counter. Her fear rose eerily into the smoky air. He saw Cadence kneeling beside the woman, wrapping her burns with dripping-wet rags. Cold water. The best way to cool down the fire-hot flesh. He dropped to his knees and peeled back an icy terry cloth.

Good. The water wasn't merely cold, it was freezing. Melting chunks from bagged ice bobbed in a bucket. Nothing more than second-degree burns, from the looks of it. She was one lucky woman. But she was frantic, beyond panic, trying to get to her babies.

"They're safe, I promise. I got them out." He said it over and over again until the woman focused on what he was saying. "They're safe, and let me take a look at your hand."

"My babies. You're sure? You're sure they're out?" She couldn't believe him. She was in shock, and rightfully so. Worse, she probably didn't feel pain from the burns, with all the adrenaline in her system. He knew about adrenaline. It was why he was moving his leg.

"I'm sure," he told her. "See? There they are, safe with those people. Here are the fire trucks. It's going to be all right. You just lie back and we'll keep cold water on these burns."

"Oh, thank God." Reason returned. Her relief became grateful tears as she refused to take her gaze from the completely unharmed children being looked after by a grandparent-type couple.

"You did good work." He removed the cloth and redunked it into the ice bucket, intending to thank the Good Samaritan who'd brought the wet towels. Not everyone helped in a crisis. But the instant his gaze met her face, the words lodged in his throat.

Cadence. He should have known it was her. She worked with her head down, intent on icing the mother's burned knee, and he noticed Cadence's slender hands. It had been more than a decade, but he would know her long sleek fingers anywhere, slender and soft. Her nails were short but painted a conservative pearled pink.

He took in the details. She wore more inexpensive items. Her cutoffs had been worn nearly white, and the T-shirt was faded from too many washings. It was hard to read the crinkled white letters proclaiming Swim For The Kids.

She was still the same old Cadence with her everything-in-its-place methodology, and she was still a bleeding heart. Swim-a-thon fund-raisers and offering aid.

Well, there was no ring on her left hand. That was something to think about as he turned to the young mother, talking to her above the screaming sirens and the air brakes of the fire trucks. The pain was probably starting to set in now. He thanked the clerk from the quick mart for a blanket and started wrapping her up.

"And you, ma'am." He offered her one of his best grins and rubbed the tears from her cheeks, gently as if she were a child. "I'm going to turn you over to the paramedics. Look, they're just pulling up now. They aren't as good-looking as I am, I'm sure." He winked. "But they'll probably be able to take good care of you."

"You're trying to make me laugh." She was sobbing harder. "You saved my babies. How can I ever thank you for that?"

"Ma'am, you don't need to thank me. I'm your tax money at work. Just doing my job." He saluted her, because it made the lines of concern wrinkling her brow ease. "You do what these men tell you, and take good care, okay? I'll be praying for you."

"Oh, thank you." More tears streaked down her face.

Ben stood, aware of Cadence's curious gaze, which he ignored. Duty first.

"What do we have here?" A young paramedic, probably around twenty by the looks of him, came up next to Ben and, with calm and knowledgeable eyes, surveyed the burned woman.

Ben filled him in quickly, so the medic could get to work. As he began to relax, he realized the fire trucks had parked and firemen were busy. The crowd had moved back to the curb, and more interested folks had gathered along the street to watch.

He was surprised to see such a peaceful scene, for he was used to patching up people with bullets flying around him. This was a piece of cake. And a happy ending all around, once the mother's burns were healed. He was thankful she hadn't been hurt worse.

But he wasn't sure what to do about Cadence. She was still talking to the mom as the paramedics began their work. He backed away, turning to make way for the medical equipment and the gurney as more paramedics arrived.

Cadence was busy. And he didn't want

to talk to her. Maybe she hadn't realized who he was, but if she did, she would not be glad to see him.

Frankly, he couldn't blame her.

Failure was something he hated, and there was so much of it in his past. Add that pain to the way his leg was killing him and the heat blast from the fire that made his back sting like crazy. It was time to go.

That's just what he did.

"Hey, wonder man, what about your burns?"

The question that came from behind him was spoken in a serene voice, as peaceful as a lazy summer's day.

Cadence's voice. The back of his neck prickled, as it did whenever he felt God at work in his life. The tingle shivered through his spine and into his soul.

She moved after him. "You're on fire. Hold still, cowboy."

She still hadn't recognized him? He waited while she covered him with the charred remains of her stadium blanket. A few pats and the embers were out, and once again he was in Cadence's debt.

Maybe this time he was man enough to know what that meant.

"Are you hurt?" she asked without looking at his face. "Your shirt has a hole in it. You've got to be burned."

"I'm okay." He turned around and braced himself for the worst.

He watched her go from polite to wide-eyed surprise. So *now* she recognized him. He hadn't been sure if she would. Not a lot of folks would these days.

Gone was the long hair of his rebellious youth, replaced by a military cut and discipline that had helped to give him an entirely new purpose to his life. When he'd known Cadence, he'd needed a purpose more than any teenaged boy wanted to admit.

Looking back wasn't easy.

Nor was it easy to watch the surprise on Cadence's lovely face turn to disdain. "Ben?"

"Yeah, it's me."

"I should have known where there was trouble, you would be nearby."

"Hey, I didn't start the fire. Blame it on static electricity."

"So it's still that way, is it? Always the other guy's fault?"

He fidgeted, definitely uncomfortable. She hadn't forgotten, that was for plumb sure, and there was no friendliness in her shimmering eyes or welcoming smile on her soft lips as she folded up the blanket.

"Your shirt's no longer smoking, so I guess you'll make it. You'll still be here to torment decent folks for some time to come."

"The good Lord willing." He cracked her his best grin, the one that seemed to have an effect on women, but she seemed impervious to it.

She didn't blink. Her stiff demeanor didn't relax. Her mouth didn't so much as twitch into an answering smile.

"What are you, a doctor?" she asked, watching him with a jaded eye.

So she wasn't glad to see him. Well, he'd known that's how she would feel, and he wasn't so glad to see her either. A doctor? No. He didn't answer, because the last thing he wanted to talk about was his life.

What about her life? What fancy city

boy had she married? What was she doing here, of all places? Guilt and regret weighed on him as he kept walking.

Some good soul had pulled his truck away from the reach of the fire—he'd left the keys in the ignition—but the driver's side was looking a little singed. Great.

Well, he didn't have the energy to get upset about it. Long ago he'd learned that disasters happened, and so he'd taken out full coverage on his insurance. Good thing, because it was a brand-new truck and had four thousand, nine hundred and, oh, about thirty miles on it the last time he'd looked.

"Are you going to have someone look at that back?" Cadence asked.

"It's nothing to worry about." He took another step and gritted his teeth. Wow, his leg was hurting worse. As if the heavyweight champion of the world had decided to take a whole lot of warm-up punches on his calf.

"Did you forget something, wonder man?"

Then it hit him. "My crutches."

"I thought you might need them. That would explain the cast on your leg." Cadence had known Ben McKaslin most of her growing-up years. This didn't surprise her. "Don't tell me it's broken and you're walking on it?"

"Walk on it? I hiked ten miles to an LZ, a landing zone, and didn't bat an eye."

Good try, but you're not impressing me, cowboy. Cadence folded her arms across her chest and did her best to glare at him. He was using that charming grin of his, the one he figured could make even the angels forget his every transgression.

She, however, was immune. Immunity gained long ago.

He reached one big hand for the crutches she held. "Contrary to popular opinion, if a fracture isn't too severe, you know, like a compound with the bone sticking through your skin, you can walk on it. Some of us are tough enough to fight bad guys, secure a perimeter and treat wounded with all sorts of ailments in spite of an injury or two."

Some things never changed, and that was Ben McKaslin. The grown man in his thirties standing before her was essentially no different from the eighteen-year-old she remembered. The one with an attitude and an overly high opinion of himself. Was she surprised? Well, she shouldn't be.

She thrust his crutches at him to keep him as far away from her as possible. "You need to have the paramedics look at your back."

"I'm good to go." He took the crutches from her, and his nearness snapped between them like static electricity.

Like the tiny spark that had ignited the gasoline fumes from the van's gas tank, the result shocked her. And had her stepping away from what had to be danger. "Your shirt's started to smolder again."

"I've had worse." He said it as if he walked through flames every day.

Ben McKaslin was everything dangerous in a man. He was too handsome, too charming, too *everything*. She'd made sure their fingers didn't touch as she handed off the crutches. The sticks of aluminum clanked as he took them in one hand, leaning now on his good leg as if the injured one was only starting to pain him just a bit.

Just like old times. Only Ben could turn a stop for gas into a three-alarm blaze, and it was never his fault. Where there was smoke, there was Ben.

Although something had changed about him, but she couldn't place what. Everyone knew he'd joined the military—and not a moment too soon, lots of folks had said. Maybe it had done him good. One could only hope. "They've got the flames out."

"So I see." He reached into his shorts pocket, leaning awkwardly on one crutch as he did it. Then he shook his head, scattering short shocks of thick dark hair. "The keys are in the truck, not my pocket. Habit."

She took one look at his dimples as he smiled more broadly, deepening them on purpose.

Right, as if he could actually charm her. She wasn't even affected. Not in the slightest. She'd learned to be strong long ago. Ben McKaslin was no man to trust. Besides, he wasn't here to stay. It was as plain as day he was injured on duty and so he'd probably be home for a visit for, what, a couple of weeks? Eight at the most, to heal that injured leg of his, and then he'd be racing back to wherever it was he was stationed.

Sure, Ben had always possessed great and admirable qualities, despite his flaws, but he wasn't a stick-around kind of man.

She was beginning to think they'd stopped making men like that sometime before she was born, because she had yet to meet one man she thought would stick. One who would be responsible and honorable enough to depend on for the long haul.

Not that she had trust issues, of course, although on many occasions, her coworkers had pointed out that she did.

Okay, so maybe she did, but her trust issues had never been the only reason he'd left the day after graduation for boot camp. And never looked back.

Forgiveness, Cadence. It was sometimes the hardest part of her faith. She'd had to do so much of it throughout her life. Maybe the angels were giving her as many opportunities as she needed to get it right.

So she tried to let her resentment go. She wasn't the head-in-the-clouds teenager she used to be. No matter how it seemed, Ben had to have matured, too. So it was with as clear a heart as she could manage that she tried one more time. "Let me take a look at your back. You can't go home like that."

"Sure I can. My family wouldn't recognize me if I didn't have something wrong."

Where he could have said those words flippantly, he was steadier. Lines had dug their way into the corners of his eyes, and gave his face character. It was his eyes that had changed. They didn't light up. They didn't sparkle.

She couldn't stop the cloying sadness that overtook her. A sense of loss overwhelmed her, and suddenly wrestling to forgive him didn't seem like such a big problem.

By the looks of it, he'd had a tough road over the years, too.

He didn't look at her as he made his explanations and his attempt at an escape and emotional distance. "I've gotta get home. Looks like they're taking the mother to the hospital. She's lucky. Goes to show a lot of folks don't realize the danger when they're filling up their tanks."

"I guess no one really thinks about it. I don't." She got the clue. He didn't want to remember old times. Neither did she. It was sad, the years that stretched empty and lost between them. As much trouble as the teenage Ben had brought into her life, he had brought laughter, too. Where once they had been close, now they couldn't be more distant. Just two people who stopped to get gas during one summer's night. They'd keep it polite, the type of conversation two strangers might have.

She didn't know what more to say to him. She didn't know how to broach the past. To ask if he'd gotten married, if he had kids, or if he'd stayed as carefree and independent as he'd always intended to be. What did he do in the military? How had he become injured?

She was so far removed from the local news. She didn't live in the same small town any longer. She lived here in Bozeman and went home a few Sunday evenings a month to have supper at her mom's, but her old life—including an innocent teenage romance with Ben—was *so* past history, it wasn't even a shadowed blip on her radar.

"Goodbye," she said to Ben casually, as if he'd never been special to her.

As if he'd never been the man she'd once intended to marry.

As if her heart were whole and her life as it should be, she walked to her car, climbed in and drove off without looking back.

Chapter Two

Cadence Chapman. Wow, that was someone he hadn't thought about in too long—
and on purpose. She could still tie him up
in knots, that was for sure. Ben rubbed the
back of his neck with one hand as he eased
the truck to a crawl.

The turnout from the paved county road
to the driveway was hard to find in the dark.
It always had been. Scrub brush, salmon-
berry bushes and super-tall thistles that had
yet to be tamed by a Weedwacker obscured
the stake marking the edge of the driveway.

The tiny red reflector still hung crooked
from the stake. It had been that way since
he was in second grade. One misty morning while waiting for the school bus, he'd

been bored, so he'd tossed rocks at the reflector, knocking it askew until one of the bigger Thornton boys had told him to stop.

There was a reason he didn't like remembering. It wasn't so good coming home. His neck was a tangle of melted-together fibers, his chest a tight ball of confused hurt, which seeing Cadence had caused even after all this time.

And on top of all that, driving up the road made his guts coil up, negating the fact that he was hungry as all get-out. He had been looking forward to raiding Rachel's refrigerator. Right now, though, until his stomach relaxed, he couldn't eat a thing. Maybe he could stay focused in the present moment—that he was just a guy coming home from the front, like so many soldiers. He'd think about the here and now, about Rachel, and wonder if she'd stayed up to meet him.

But the past reached out to grab him like a ghost in the dark as he bumped up the gravel driveway through the cottonwoods and over the rush of the creek. Images from long ago, grown fuzzy and dim with time—of a happy boy, in the days before he'd been an orphan, wading in the water watching tadpoles and little trout and searching for deer tracks.

He slid down the windows just to hear the wind and the water gurgling and the whisper of the small green leaves in the night air. He couldn't stay in the present. Too many memories came with the sounds of the breeze. Darker memories came, of how he'd hidden in the culvert after his parents had been killed in a car accident, and no one could find him.

No, that wasn't such a good memory.

Ben hit the control and the windows zipped up, cutting off the night, shutting off the memories and banishing the past.

But not entirely. The past was hard to erase. It was tenacious, and it lurked behind him like the shadows. As the truck rolled and bounced up the driveway, he realized the private lane was in terrible shape. It could use a grading and a new layer of gravel. Maybe he'd help Rachel with that. He desperately latched on to any normal thought as the truck careened the last few yards to the lone house on the hill.

The house was a neat rancher built when

his parents had been alive, on a five-acre tract on the good side of town and along the river on the back of the property, within sight of the elementary school and the park. But right now it was nearly pitch-black. The only light to guide him was a small spill of porch light over the front door.

Rachel had left it on for him. He warmed up at his sister's thoughtfulness. That hadn't changed, nor had the tall leafy maples, older than he was, which stood at attention like gigantic sentries around the yard.

Rachel knew he was coming. They were the closest in age. She was less than two years his junior and seemed to understand him, if anyone ever could. She always made him feel comfortable without judging his shortcomings. And instead of scolding him on the phone for his sudden visit, she'd sounded truly happy, and not put out that he was springing a visit on her.

"I can't wait to see you, and, hey, you're getting better! Last time you called from the airport."

"See? I can be taught."

"The door is always open. It's your home, too." Her voice had dipped with emotion, and he closed off his heart and memory.

How did he tell his sweet and wonderful sister that he didn't want a home? That's why he was more nomad than anything, and she was the one who lived in the family's house. She clung to the past as if it were something to be treasured, not forgotten.

Well, he was more than happy to forget, but not his sisters.

Rachel was probably asleep, or possibly reading in bed, since her bedroom was on the other side of the house. Affection stretched like a rubber band in his chest. His sisters sure worked hard, and he knew that Rachel often covered the morning shifts at the family restaurant in town, so she got to bed pretty early to be on the job by six.

The clock in the truck's dashboard told him it was well after midnight. Yeah, he thought as he pulled up to the closed double garage doors and killed the engine. She definitely had given up waiting for him.

That was okay. He was beat. He'd be lousy company anyway. It had been a long drive from Pensacola and his back hurt, but not as badly as his leg.

He gritted his teeth as he tried to move. Oh, yeah, the adrenaline was wearing off, all right. He was too tough to admit it, so he tried to ignore the streak and throb of pain that felt as if he'd been shot in the calf with a bullet. Wait—that's exactly what had happened to him.

Talk about luck. He still had his leg, so he didn't care how much it hurt. He'd treated lots of guys who hadn't been as fortunate. As he climbed out of the cab and transferred weight onto his good leg, he pushed aside the pain and stiffness and breathed in the silence.

Whoa, he'd forgotten how peaceful it could be here. There was no tracer fire, no beat of chopper blades and no rat-tat-tat of machine guns. Trouble was half a world away.

God, don't let me be here for long.

"Go home. Rest up. Go fishing or something," his colonel had told him. "When your med leave is up, we'll see if we need to cross train you into another job."

No way. His guts clenched. He'd get this leg back into shape, he vowed with all his might as his feet stepped on the dependable Montana earth. *Right, God?*

But no answer came on the temperate warmth of the sweet summer air. Well, he wasn't going to let that trouble him. He was determined. And he was home, for better or worse. He let the wind pummel him as he took a look around. So much wide-open space.

He'd been back for holidays when he was in the country. But that usually meant he was huddled in the house on the bitter Thanksgiving and Christmas nights while it snowed, busy catching up on the family news, eating cookies and telling tall tales. He'd always had a hundred different things on his mind when he'd been here visiting.

Besides, he avoided peace on purpose.

His M.O. always was to stay a few days, and then he was gone. Whether he was visiting here or on a quick break in his duplex at Eglin Air Force Base, he was always rushing off to strife in some part of the world, where strong men with guns kept this country safe. He was proud to be one of those men.

I'm anxious to get back, God, he prayed, studying the velvet tapestry of the night sky. *Please heal me up quick.*

He hauled out his crutches—he hated the dumb things—and tried to keep their clattering to a minimum. If he couldn't go back to his work, he didn't know what he'd do. He'd spent the last and best part of his life as a pararescue jumper, a PJ, stationed on bases around the world—Japan, Korea, Italy and, of course, the Middle East.

And since special ops was his thing, he did a lot of work beneath the night skies. Somewhere under a sky like this, his team was at work without him, pumped full of adrenaline, fast roping from a Blackhawk or checking gear in preparation for a high-altitude jump. Then they'd set up and secure a perimeter, and proceed with their mission. Often rescuing a downed pilot behind enemy lines or liberating captured American soldiers.

I miss it, he thought as he opened the

club cab door. He'd been out of the field for six weeks—one in the hospital and five hanging around his duplex looking out at the Gulf of Mexico. Watching other soldiers gear up and head out, leaving him behind.

I'd give anything to be dodging bullets. His being ached with the wish, but he'd learned a long time ago wishes got you exactly nothing. Only hard work did.

And that's why he was here. He leaned heavily on his crutches. The silent glide of an owl winging across the span of sky was awesome. He waited while the bird disappeared behind the tall maples.

He felt the change before he heard the faintest sound. Instinct had him whipping toward the front porch, where the doorknob began to rasp as it moved.

Then came a light step—a woman's—and the scrape of the solid wood door over the threshold. The hinges gave a tiny squeal, and he knew it was Rachel before she stepped into sight. The single sconce fixture showered light over her like liquid brilliance.

It's good to see you, little sister. She had

a sweetheart's face, big blue eyes and cheekbones that supermodels would envy. The breeze brought her faint scent of vanilla fragrance and the intake of her surprised gasp when she spotted him behind the pickup.

"Is that a no-good burglar lurking out on the driveway?" As pure as spun sugar, Rachel hurried toward him wearing her big baggy pj's and slippers—in summer. She was always cold, it seemed.

Her long brown hair hid part of her face as she swept toward him, the shuffling of the fabric beneath her feet distinctive on the aggregate concrete walk. "Oh, wait, it's just you. My hero of a brother!"

"That's not me. A hero? No, you must be talking about someone else."

"You'll always be a hero to me." She held out her arms, rushing toward him for a hug.

It was impossible not to adore her and, truth be told, she was his favorite sister—not that a guy was supposed to have favorites, but Rachel could steal even his heart made of stone.

He pulled her close, feeling how much

he liked being her big brother. And when she bounded back to get a good look at him, shadows settled into her face and deep in her gaze.

He shivered, because Rachel had a knack for seeing too much. "You're a lovely sight for these sore eyes, darlin'. You cut your hair since Christmas."

"Just trimmed it a little. Look at you, all banged up." Her words were light, but the steady appraisal she gave him was anything but. Sheer sisterly adoration lit her up.

And humbled him. "I'm not all that, little sister. I dodged left when I should have dodged right, and look at me."

"Sporting a fashionable cast and two aluminum sticks. Are you in any pain? Let me get that bag for you—"

"Take the smaller one. Lift the rucksack and you'll pop a disk. It's heavy." He could have predicted she wasn't about to listen until she grabbed hold of the sack's heavy-duty handles and heaved with an unlady-like groan. The bag didn't budge.

"See? I told you."

"All right. I'll take the smaller bag, but

don't think I'm going to let you out of this so easily. You told us that you had *minor* injuries. Minor injuries, my foot! Look at you!"

"These are minor injuries. Compared to the other guys." The truth was his job was about as dangerous as it got in the military and he'd been eerily lucky to haven gotten out of that particular situation with his leg intact.

As he hefted the heavy sack from behind the seat, he took a second to silently give thanks again for what could only have been divine intervention on that mission. It had been as if an angel had nudged him the few extra inches out of harm's way, saving his leg but also his life, his career and his sanity. What were a few weeks in Montana compared to that?

"Well, there are no bullets here, tough guy. I'm just glad you're home."

She led the way along the walk, glancing over her shoulder constantly to check on his progress, her sharp eyes watching for any signs of his pain. She held the door wide for him, after leaning inside to flip on the light. "I knew you were coming, so it's no excuse, but the house is a mess. I apologize."

"You've gone from not picking up your room to not picking up your house?"

"Something like that." Eyes twinkling, she waited until he was in the entry hall before closing the door tight and throwing the bolt.

The big house seemed to echo around them, all darkness and empty-sounding rooms. She carried his bag down the hall, but he couldn't seem to follow her. Memories threatened his well-defended perimeter, but he managed to battle them back. Rachel had made a lot of changes to their childhood home over the years, but still, he remembered.

All he had to do was to look at the fireplace of smooth gray river rock that reached for two stories toward the vaulted ceiling, and he saw the past. Once Dad's animal trophies had been proudly displayed there. The five-point buck and the three-point elk were long gone, replaced by clear twinkle lights Rachel left up all year round. But memory was a fluid thing, and he blinked back the past.

I'm tired, that's all, he told himself as he let the awkward rucksack slide from his shoulder and smack to the carpet. He propped his crutches against the wall of stone and dropped into the sectional. Dozens of little frilly throw pillows nearly suffocated him.

"Do you have enough of these frilly things?" He tossed a half dozen of them across the cluttered coffee table into the deep cushions of a big overstuffed chair.

"Sorry, you're in a girl zone, remember? It might be a hardship for a big tough guy like you. It's not camouflage or military motif, but trust me, eyelet, lace and ribbons won't hurt you."

"I can't relax around this stuff." He sent a pale pink pillow with a satin heart sailing across the room. "You're up late. Is there something I can do for you?"

"Ah, find me the secret to time travel so I can go back to this morning and start over," came her response from down the hall.

Yeah, she worked too hard, and he didn't like it. She was gone a suspiciously long time for just dropping off his bag.

"You're not doing stuff for me like making up a bed, are you?"

"Oh, no, I already did that. I can't imagine how tired you have to be. I've got a plate keeping warm in the oven. I thought you might be hungry." Rachel waltzed into sight.

You are the one who looks exhausted, little sister. He hated the dark rings beneath her eyes, but she managed a real smile.

"You're tired, Rache. Go to bed. Stop worrying over me. Stop doing things for me. You have enough to do as it is, and I can take care of myself."

"Yes, I know, you're a big tough Special Forces soldier. But you don't know how worried we've all been. Ever since we were told you were missing in action—" The lovely soft pink in her face disappeared, and in the faint light she looked snow-white. Pain twisted across her face. "I was scared for you."

Just like that, she got behind his steel defenses. He hated the fact that she'd been worried. "I wasn't missing. Not in the true sense of the word. I knew exactly where I was."

"Yes, but we didn't, hence the 'missing' part. And I did miss you. I was worried to death."

"No, I was misplaced for a while, nothing more."

Rachel wasn't fooled. Her eyes filled with tears and she was suddenly in his arms—his sweet little sister who'd always seemed so fragile, and here she was crying over him when he was perfectly fine. Over him, when there had been so many others who hadn't come out of the ambush alive.

"You're wasting your tears, you know." He tried to be gruff.

She swiped the dampness from her cheeks and pushed away from him, leaving him with a hole the size of the state of Montana in his chest. Wishing he knew what to do or what to say. Wishing he knew how to stick. He was a horrible big brother, and he was at a loss as to how to fix it.

He'd do anything to protect and provide for his sisters, but the truth was simple: he wasn't good at relationships. He was better at bailing out—staying away—than at being here. He liked to keep an arm's distance from intimacy, and he never shared the real Ben McKaslin. Not with Rachel.

Not with anyone.

He kept relationships simple and on the surface. It was easy to do when he lived so far away. All he had to do was send quick letters with funny anecdotes, e-mail with jokes, that kind of thing. But here in person, when he had to relate face-to-face, that's where he felt how closed off he'd become. He didn't know what to do about it or how to fix it.

Maybe he didn't want to. He liked being alone. It suited him.

Rachel, who had no such problems showing her emotions, tugged a tissue from the box on the coffee table and swiped the dampness from her eyes. "You don't understand how scared I was for you. I thought you'd never come back."

"Don't you waste your tears on me." So he wasn't a tough guy all the time. "I do what I do in the military so you can sleep safe in your bed at night."

"I'd like you to be safe, too."

"I am. I've got my M-203."

"I take it that's a gun?"

"One of the best. Stop worrying, got it?"

"Yeah." She sighed, as if in resignation, and opened her mouth as if she were going to argue, then decided against it. She sniffed, dabbing at her eyes as she trailed off in the direction of the dark kitchen.

One thing he wasn't going to let her do was wait on him. He wasn't that hurt—or so he kept telling himself. He leaned forward to reach for the crutches, and the springs beneath him protested.

"I hear you trying to get up and don't you dare!" Rachel scolded from the kitchen. "Stay right where you are, okay? I'll bring supper to you. We had a slow night at the diner, so I had time to really cook up a big plate of your favorites."

"I told you not to go to any trouble."

"What trouble? Now, what do you want to drink? I bought chocolate milk at the store today, since I knew you were coming. A big gallon all for you."

"All for me? That must mean you have your own stash of chocolate milk in the fridge you're hiding from me."

"If I don't, then you'll drink every last

drop, just like you do every time you stay with me. I've learned my lesson."

"Hey, I buy more for you."

"You do. I couldn't ask for a better brother." She was back, bringing her gentle cheer and a foil-covered plate with her.

Her words touched him, and he was again at a loss to return the sentiment. Not that he didn't feel it, just that…he couldn't say something so vulnerable.

Pretending it was the food that mattered, he took the plate from her, hot pad and all, and tore off the foil. The mouth-watering scents of country fried chicken, gravy and buttermilk biscuits made his stomach growl. That was much easier to deal with than his feelings. "This is great. I owe you supper tomorrow."

"It's a deal. And if you noticed, I gave you three helpings of mashed potatoes." She set a wrapped napkin of flatware on the coffee table along with the carton of milk.

When he leaned forward to grab the napkin, her eyes rounded. His shirt—he'd forgotten all about his back, since his leg hurt worse than a first-degree burn.

Rachel went to her knees. "Oh, what did you do? Your shirt is singed and there's this big hole. Were you on fire?"

"Yep, but it was nothing you need to worry about." He forked in a mound of buttery potato, so creamy and rich, and kept talking with his mouth full. Man, he was hungry. "Disaster finds me."

"As long as it doesn't find you anymore. Do you need a salve or something? A bandage?"

She looked dismayed, and over something so minor. It was nice to know how much she cared. The dark circles beneath her eyes seemed even darker, if that were possible, and she radiated exhaustion.

The last thing she needed to do was waste any more effort on him, when she was what really mattered. Rachel and Amy and Paige were all the family he had in this world. "You look ready to drop, little sister. Go to bed, get some sleep and have good dreams. Will you do that for me?"

"I am bushed, but you're on crutches."

"I'm capable. I'll be fine. Trust me." He waited while her internal debate played across her face. Rachel was so easy to read.

Always good-hearted and caring. It was a knack he wished he had, but he did his best to return what she'd already given to him. "Do I have to haul you over my shoulder and carry you down the hall?"

"Nope. I'll go, if you're sure you don't need me."

"You're driving me crazy." He said the words kindly, because he'd come to appreciate true goodness in the world, for it was rare. Her thoughtfulness said everything. She'd gone to all this trouble for him.

Yeah, he was pretty fond of her, too. "You didn't happen to have any pie in the kitchen?"

"I'll never tell. You'll have to raid the fridge to find out." Her eyes twinkled, eyes so like Mom's. She looked more like Mom as time went by, and seeing that hurt.

Rachel waved as she breezed down the hallway.

"Good night, Rache."

"Good night, big brother. Oh! Should I take your bag to your room, since I'm headed in that direction?"

"Nah, don't bother. I can stow it."

"Of course you can—what was I thinking?" She rolled her eyes, and she looked as if she were biting the inside of her cheek to keep from laughing at him. "I forget that you're tough."

Not tough enough. If he were made of titanium, then maybe he would be. But the sense of failure and regret surrounded him. His parents' deaths. The lost and angry boy he'd become. The teenager on a self-destructive course. The people he'd hurt—his sisters, his aunt and uncle.

And Cadence. She'd looked beautiful tonight, strong and confident. Probably wildly successful in her life—but he could see in her the Montana country girl she used to be.

He was proud of her. She'd made something great of her life. See? She had been loads better off without him. He'd made the right decision long ago—for his own reasons, sure, but still. It had been right for her, too. He'd been able to get out of this quicksand town, and she'd realized her dreams of Olympic gold. Yeah, he'd watched her win on TV. He'd been stationed in Japan at the time, and he'd violated direct orders to watch her perfect dive.

Why was running into Cadence tonight part of God's plan for him? His heart wrenched. What use was it in seeing what he could have had? In seeing the man he should have been?

Failure wrapped around him and he pushed the plate away. He sat in the dark and silence for a long while.

Chapter Three

It was gonna be a hot one. Sweat was already gathering between her shoulder blades as the morning sun, barely over the rim of the Bridger Mountains, beat down on her back.

Cadence balanced her cup of chai tea in her left hand and rummaged around in the bottom of her bag. She moved aside her rolled towels, her change of clothes, a paperback book, a lifeguard's whistle and her wallet.

Loose change chimed and chinked together on the bottom of the bag as she felt her way to the fuzzy ball attached to her key ring—there it was. She tugged and yanked, and the key ring came free. One

day she was going to have to get better or-
ganized—or clean out the bottom of her
bag. But not today. The little soft stuffed
sunshine with a black smiley face dangling
from the key ring grinned up at her as she
sorted through the keys.

One day I'll have enough time to be or-
ganized and together. But for now, she was
just doing her best.

She unlocked the door and let it click
shut behind her. Late, late, late. Swimmers
were going to start showing up any minute.
She hurried through the echoing building,
flicking on lights. Her flip-flops snapped
against the concrete floor and her steps re-
verberated in the high ceiling overhead.

For now, she loved her life. She loved
starting her days here, opening up the public pool. The sharp scent of chlorinated water
was oddly comforting to her, and the smell
relaxed her more than a big cup of steaming
chamomile tea at night ever could. The
aroma always brought up the best memories
of when she'd been training and competing.

And now teaching and coaching. There
were a lot of bad memories, too, but they
were easy to set aside when she was here,

the only one in this huge building. The water seemed to be waiting for her, and the morning sun streamed through the upper windows in the cathedral ceiling to sparkle and dance on the pool's surface.

Stop dallying, Cadence! You're late, late, late!

She dumped her stuff on the office counter, slipped out of her comfy T-shirt and stowed her things in a private locker in the back.

The quiet slosh of the water against the tile sides and the echo of it in the rafters drew her, as it always did. No matter where life had taken her or the hardships she'd been privileged to face, this place was her home, and she didn't know what she'd do without her swimming.

Thank You, Father, she prayed as she touched the humble gold cross at her throat, *for this passion in my life.* Without her swimming and the sanctuary of places like this, where would she be? Living a desperate life like her sister? Abusing drugs and alcohol like her brother?

Her future might not have turned out as rosy as she'd planned, but she was grateful for this morning and for this path she was walking.

The somber black hands on the big clock above the office stretched toward five-thirty. Yikes. She had a few minutes to get the lights on and the ropes up. The regulars would forgive her for being a few minutes late, but she wouldn't.

Moving fast, she stepped out of her nylon shorts and, without needing to think about it, raised her arms and cut into the cool water. Ah, a piece of heaven on earth, she thought as the wonderful glide of the water slicked her swimsuit to her skin and she sliced to the surface.

Scissor kicking, she let the water sluice down her face as she reached out and grabbed the rope by feel. As she did every morning, she uncoiled it, let the bobbins laze on the water. Swimming all out, she worked fast to uncoil the next rope, took each hook firmly in her hands and leaned back, letting the water carry her.

A few powerful kicks and she was floating in the middle of the Olympic-sized pool. A few more and she was nearly across, working to keep the ropes tangle free and straightening out. At the far end of the pool she latched them up, working quickly as the clock stroked to 5:27.

At the front door there was a rattle that ricocheted like a bullet through the high rafters—and it kept coming.

Who was that impatient? Her regulars knew one knock would bring her running if she were a little behind, like this morning. But someone was very persistent. Okay, so she was now a minute later. She set up the last two lane ropes, climbed out of the pool and, dripping wet, yanked open the front door.

There, illuminated by the bold strokes of the rising sun, stood a solid six feet of man. Right away, she noticed the military short black hair and linebacker's shoulders. This impatient morning swimmer leaned on a pair of crutches and his handsome, rugged features twisted from impatience to what could only be described as dismay as he recognized her.

Ben? Her heart gave a sudden jump and took off racing. What was he doing here? For some inexplicable reason her tongue had stopped working and she could only stare at him, the way he was staring at her. She couldn't focus on anything or anyone else, even though she was vaguely aware the benches along the walkway were occupied.

The early-morning regulars began to move closer. She distantly recognized the two gray-haired men who were faithful lap swimmers—per orders from their doctors. Fit and quick, they were the next to reach the double doors.

"Morning, Cadence. We started to worry, since it's not like you to be more than a few minutes late, on the rare occasions that you are." Arnold Mays was the first to the door. "Is everything all right?"

"Y-yes, thank you." She had more problems with her sister, but that was nothing to trouble these fine people with. As for Ben...

Chester Harrison halted beside Arnold, his best friend for over sixty years, and nodded once in the direction of Ben McKaslin. "He's an eager one. Son, you're doing pretty good with those crutches."

"I try not to let anything get in my way." Ben stood straight and strong despite his injuries.

The men moved inside, talking about sports as they went.

In the clear light of day he seemed very different from the boy she remembered. He looked like an entirely different man, someone made of unbowed steel. He shrugged away his injuries as if they were nothing.

Her gaze slid to his cast; it was a light-weight removable one. His leg was injured, but it must be healing, she figured, remembering how he'd managed to walk on it. Of course, he'd come to swim—one of the best rehabilitation methods for injured limbs.

He was a customer, no more. This wasn't personal. She held the door wide and tried to avoid his gaze. "C'mon in."

Ben remained where he stood, off to the side of the doorway, the wind ruffling his short dark hair like freshly mown grass. This morning he wore cutoffs and an old wash-worn tank top that bore some fading military insignia.

A small duffel hung from his shoulder, barely visible, since he'd shoved it behind him so he could use his crutches. His big feet were hidden in a pair of ratty sneakers. Ben was never one for putting much stock in appearance, and after all this time she finally understood.

It was the man and not the clothes she wondered about while she greeted Harriet Oleson, who sprinted along the walkway from the parking lot. Spry at ninety-three, the ever-young Mrs. Oleson praised the beautiful morning as she dashed by, eager to start her laps.

Alone with Ben. The breeze carried with it the faint scent of smoke—either from the fields burning off or the wildfire in the nearby national forest that had started during the night somewhere south of town.

Cadence waited while a muscle ticked along Ben's iron jaw. "Are you coming in or not? I've got to be on deck."

"This is the lap swim, right? Open to anyone?"

"Well, theoretically. I suppose that includes you. Or maybe it's the lifeguard you have a problem with."

"No." He hooked his crutches more firmly beneath his arms and strode through the door, moving with the determination of a marathon runner sighting the finish line. He left her holding the door, watching his back.

He was so…calm. That was a change from the boy she remembered. He walked straight and strong, as if nothing could diminish him.

"'Mornin', Cadence." Jessie, another regular and a young mom in a hurry, had news of the approaching wildfire. They spoke for a few seconds as Ben disappeared. Jessie soon raced off to get changed, and Cadence was needed poolside.

The office wasn't empty as she passed through, stopping to grab her cup of tea. She greeted the assistant guard, a college girl named Melody, who must have come in the back door. She looked exhausted from what had to be another late night of studying. Melody resumed counting out change in the cash register's till.

As she did every morning, Cadence unlocked the locker-room doors, the gentlemen first because she knew Chester and Arnold would be showered down and waiting. And they were, pushing out the door and hurrying to pick their lane. Their bare feet slapped along the deck to the shallow end.

Ben was still on her mind as she paced the length of the pool to unlock the women's rooms. She exchanged words with Harriet, who was good to go as she slipped on her swimming cap and made her way to her favorite lane.

This was the rhythm to Cadence's morning routine, a comforting sameness that seemed to start a day out right. Above the splashes and quiet talk of the swimmers, she slipped her shorts over her wet suit, climbed up on her chair and let the warm spicy tea soothe her.

There had been times in her past when she'd never believed she could be this content. The little girl with big dreams and ambition hadn't grown up to live an important life in sports broadcasting. That little girl she'd been had nearly lost every dream.

But Ben McKaslin? What about the rebellious renegade boy with long hair and a mile-wide self-destructive bent? What had become of his dreams?

There he was, coming from the locker

rooms on his crutches, his skin bronzed as if he'd spent most of the year in the sun. He appeared so well muscled she thought that he must put in serious workout time every day.

Wearing long navy blue trunks that looked like military issue, he leaned his crutches against the wall, out of the way. He limped to one of the nearby benches and sat, then ripped off the Velcro tabs of the cast as if there was nothing wrong with his leg whatsoever. Intent on his task, he didn't look her way.

He's the past, she reminded herself, and continued to scan the diligent swimmers. They were already hard at work, with their heads down and skimming through the water. Ben slipped into the pool, choosing an empty lane, reached out with his strong arms and took off, favoring his injured leg as he swam a perfect, fast, efficient crawl stroke.

She couldn't watch him and not remember the too-fierce, too-energetic and larger-than-life McKaslin boy who had made chaos out of nothing.

Trouble still followed him like a shadow,

if last night was a clue. He seemed so remote. He seemed so bitter. She hadn't been able to get him out of her mind through the night, making sleep nearly impossible. And now here he was in her pool, more distant and silent than he'd been at the gas station.

Why does seeing him make me hurt, Lord? It was as if she saw her past when she looked at him. Not just the sweet way she'd loved him, in the most idealistic sense, but more. Seeing him made her assess her life and the years gone by.

She was no longer the girl who believed in gold medals and honorable people and that if she worked hard, lived faithfully and did the right thing, then only good things would come her way.

For a long while she'd been disillusioned. She'd felt as if God had betrayed her by letting her chase dreams that would only bring her sorrow. But then she saw it was simply part of growing up. Of putting away childish things, and a child's dreamy view of the world. Of a world that was not fair, not kind and not safe, and learning to do right in that world.

I'm no longer in love with you, Ben

McKaslin. When she should have felt relieved, she felt only more jumbled inside. More confused—and how could that be possible? Because the old Ben, the young boy, was gone, too.

He'd always had a noble spirit, and as a young idealistic girl she'd seen the best in him—when he had been trying to find the worst in himself. Had he succeeded in that sad endeavor? Or, instead, had he found the best?

She took another sip of tea and put away the questions. Ben McKaslin's life wasn't her business, and maybe that was for the best.

She closed the door to the past and concentrated on the moment. On the contented splish and rush of the swimmers in the water, of the gurgle of the pump sucking water through the filter, and of the bobbins on the rope slapping against the tile on the far end of the pool.

This moment. This is what mattered. She purposely kept herself from noticing how he soared through the water like a dolphin.

He's not special to me anymore…he's a stranger.

She took another sip of tea, climbed down from her chair and paced the long way around the pool, taking her time, so that when she came around to him, he was exactly in the middle of his lane.

Think of him as just another swimmer.

She took refuge in the corner, where she kept a sharp eye on everything, even on this quiet morning where it seemed nothing could go wrong.

She'd learned the hard way that's when devastation happened—when you least expected it.

His leg was killing him, but would he show weakness? No way. Not in front of anyone, especially Cadence. Clutching the wall, he paused long enough to catch his breath and watched her out of his peripheral vision.

Every fiber of his being seemed aware of the way she moved like sunlight around the huge Olympic-sized pool. Her uniform, a lifeguard's nylon windbreaker and matching shorts over her swimsuit, made the moment loop oddly back in time. They had both spent a lot of time in this pool as teenaged kids.

We've both traveled long, divergent roads since.

As he kicked away from the wall, feeling the water slide over his skin, he stretched out into a steady breaststroke so he could keep his eyes barely above water level and watch Cadence as she circled the pool.

How weird was it that she was working here? *Working.* As a lifeguard. What had happened to her big plans to get out of this backwater place? What about the fame and riches of her diving career? Why wasn't she in broadcast sports?

Good questions. He remembered what the doc had told him—the one he'd nearly blown a gasket at because he hadn't liked the diagnosis. *You can't always get what you want, hotshot.* The M.D.'s words haunted him as he touched the wall and began another lap. Had the same thing happened to Cadence?

It troubled him all through his laps. When white-hot pain was shooting through his calf and he was clenching his jaw so tight he couldn't breathe correctly between strokes, he had to call it a day. Done.

And after only a quarter of a mile, too. He swallowed the disappointment as he climbed out of the pool, ignoring the stabbing pain and the throbbing burn of injured muscles and tendons. He hadn't pushed as hard as he'd wanted to, and he was beat. Recovery might not be as quick as he'd hoped.

You have to be tougher, that's all.

Ben ignored the way his leg was shaking so hard, it wouldn't support any weight. He was glad Cadence was at the far end of the pool—he'd timed it that way. She stood by the diving pool, separated by a concrete bridge from the regular pool. The diving boards towered behind her, the springboard and platforms empty and still.

For an instant the image of Cadence on TV accepting her medal was superimposed on her standing poolside in her jacket and suit, with her silver whistle hanging around her neck.

He still couldn't reconcile the two images as she moved on ordinary, discount-store flip-flops along the deck, squatting down with the grace of a gymnast to speak with the elderly lady who'd passed him about six times in the next lane.

Whatever happened to Cadence is none of your business, man.

Ben snatched his crutches and settled them into place. The deck was aggregate concrete, which provided decent traction for his crutches, but it was slightly wet in places from folks dripping on their way from the showers to the pool. He went slowly.

More devoted swimmers were arriving—it looked as if he'd stopped at just the right time. He'd been all right swimming slowly and steadily, but he'd been in a lane by himself. If he'd stayed in the pool longer, he wouldn't have been able to keep pace.

His pride burned as he headed to the locker-room door on his crutches. He'd remember to be here the same time—when they opened—tomorrow. And Cadence, would she be on duty?

Keeping his face down, he risked glancing upward through his lashes to watch her. What had happened to Cadence to bring her here, when she'd had everything she'd ever wanted? While he turned the corner and moved into the showers, he remembered her teenaged voice, soft and sweet. *I can't wait to get out of this boringville. I'm getting out and I'm never coming back.*

Never was one of those ominous words, Ben had learned. Because we weren't as in control of our lives as we liked to think. God was, and Ben had no clue why the Lord had brought him back here to the central Montana country where he'd been born and raised.

He was lucky—he had nothing to complain about. His primary duty in the military was rescuing and patching up pilots and soldiers wounded in action, wherever they were, on the front lines or in hostile enemy territory. He'd seen enough wounded men and women to know that for whatever reason, the angels had been keeping him safe on his last mission, but he couldn't help feeling defeated.

I can't do any good to anyone here, Father. He was impatient and he knew it, and he believed that this, too, was part of God's plan for him, but he was impatient anyway. Duty called. He'd had to turn off the radio again this morning on the drive here because there had been an update about soldiers being shot and injured in Iraq.

Pararescue had been Ben's purpose for all of his adult life. He was just irritable, being stuck here. Irritable waiting to get his leg back into shape.

Whatever had happened to bring Cadence back couldn't have been too traumatic, he decided as he showered and limped to the lockers. She'd looked great—more relaxed, her smile easy and wide, and her cornflower-blue eyes sparkling as she'd talked with her morning regulars.

Whatever happened, he'd be seeing her again. But they were strangers now. There was no going back to their high school days when they'd been practically inseparable. When he'd loved her with the whole of his heart. When he'd believed they were soul mates.

No such things as soul mates, he told himself as he pulled his T-shirt over his head. Failure became a tight vise in his chest until it hurt to breathe. He'd failed at every major relationship he'd ever started, and he knew he'd failed Cadence the most.

Just go chase your gold, he'd said to her selfishly, hoping to hurt her, in the way that only an eighteen-year-old boy could.

Seeing her brought back too much pain. There were other times, aside from early mornings, set aside at the pool for lap swims. Maybe he'd start coming in the evening.

Chapter Four

"Ben!" His sister Amy saw him first, since she was ringing up a ticket behind the front counter. She handed Mr. Brisbane his change and came around the corner with both arms outstretched. "I heard a rumor you were in town. Oh, give me a hug, mister!"

"Do I have to?" He groaned, but he was only faking it, and they both knew it. His baby sister was all grown up—and happy, judging by the glow on her cheeks and her wide smile.

Wow. Since when did Amy smile like that? He snuggled her to him and gave her a raspberry on the side of her head, something he'd done since she was a baby toddling around. And his chest warmed when she laughed, the sound making him feel as if he were finally home.

"Look how healthy you look!" Amy swatted him in the chest with the flat of her hand, a playful swipe.

So many emotions swarmed within him, seeing her so happy and grown up and centered, as if she'd come into her place in the world.

She stepped back to get a good look at him. "You scared us all to death. Missing in action. Then a casualty."

He could see she was prepared to go on, but he held up his hand. "I've already gotten the lecture from Rachel. I promise, no more getting shot on duty."

"Ben." Mr. Brisbane had pocketed his wallet, and offered his hand. "It's good to see you back in one piece, son. Hoo-yah."

"Thank you, sir." Ben saluted the former soldier, who'd fought in the Pacific and been wounded on Iwo Jima. "It's good to see you again."

With a nod as if to say, "You'll do, Ben McKaslin," Ed Brisbane moved on, and behind him was another veteran. Clyde

Winkler had braved the beaches at Normandy.

"You make us proud, son." Clyde clapped Ben on the shoulder as he passed, as if unable to say more.

Proud? No, Ben figured he'd been passable as a soldier, but when he looked up, leaning on his crutches to follow Amy down the aisle to the closest empty booth, everyone in the diner was on their feet.

And clapping.

They weren't applauding him specifically, he knew, but just that he was the nearest soldier from the Iraqi conflict. The Middle East was so far away, where so many men and women served—soldiers who'd left their homes, families and lives behind to serve and protect. Ben thought of the soldiers he hadn't been able to save. Of the men and women who'd given their lives for their country.

He blushed and felt inadequate. "Don't clap because I didn't dodge a bullet. That's not the kind of behavior you want to reward."

A ripple of laughter rolled through the diner. Grateful he didn't have to walk a step farther, he collapsed on the seat and let Amy steal his crutches.

"Coffee." She returned to pour him a cup. Her diamond engagement ring glittered in the cheerful sunlight slanting through the window.

Had it been a month since she'd e-mailed him with her news? She'd been excited to be engaged. His sister. The one who didn't trust men. She must have found a trustworthy one—or one she thought was an upstanding kind of guy.

We'll have to see about that. He reached for the sugar canister. "Where is he? Is he on the grill?"

"No, Heath's getting some paperwork straightened out. He's a doctor, but he has to pass the state qualifications. Do you want the huckleberry pancake platter?"

His favorite. He knew he really was here, because home was where they knew you, and loved you anyway. "Sure."

"Comin' right up, brother dear." She padded her way up the aisle, light on her feet, pausing to refill cups and chat with the regulars.

An odd time warp overtook him. It was

as if nothing had changed in all the years he'd been gone. Since he was a little guy no taller than the tables, he'd done time in this diner. The white tile floor was the same, the big drafty front windows were the same, the worn red Formica tabletops, too. The same families and customers had been frequenting this diner for two generations.

The years seemed to slip away until he felt like the kid he used to be grumbling over the hot grill, angry that his fate in life was to have been born in a family that owned a diner. Not a health club or a yacht or a recording studio in Los Angeles, but a dull little restaurant in the middle of Nowhere, Montana.

It wasn't shame he felt. It wasn't sadness at the lost boy he'd been. But his vision doubled, as if he'd taken a blow to the head. Regrets washed through him like acid rain, eating at his core. He'd come a long way from the angry, rebellious boy he'd been.

In the air force he knew who he was. Master Sergeant McKaslin, squad leader, a pararescuer who'd been on every continent on this planet—except Antarctica.

He'd rescued downed pilots and injured soldiers from live combat and hostage situations and delivered lifesaving medical care. From deserts and jungles and hot zones all around the globe. He knew who he was in his uniform.

But here, in this town he'd grown up in, he was a stranger. He was not the same Ben McKaslin who'd left at eighteen. That's why every rare visit home was tough. *How am I going to make it six more weeks?*

"Ben? Is that you?" A familiar voice rose among the din of the diner behind him.

Paige. His throat ached at the sight of the woman who'd been both big sister and step-in mom when he'd needed it most. He hated to think where he'd be without her guidance long ago. Or maybe her guidance had come more out of her desperation, since he hadn't been the easiest teenage boy to deal with.

She hadn't changed much. She'd let her hair grow past her shoulders, although this morning it was swept back out of the way. Her arms were around him before he could

register the finer lines that had cut into her
face. Tiny ones around her dark eyes and
around the corners of her mouth.

Time. It was passing. Paige was a handful of years older than he was. And although she was somehow lovelier than
ever, it reminded him that they were all
getting older. He'd done the right thing in
coming home.

He'd given the ten-second allotment for
acts of affection and he stiffened, drawing
back, though he couldn't deny he liked
being fussed over by his sisters. "I'm a
Special Forces soldier. I don't do hugs."

"Suffer anyway. They train you for receiving torture, right?" She gave him an
extra squeeze, which was supposedly more
torture, he figured, before releasing him.
Happiness crinkled the corners of her eyes.
"Oh, you look good. What's with the
crutches? You weren't tough enough to
take a bullet without getting hurt?"

"I could take grenade shrapnel and a
claymore that didn't go off good enough,
but I wasn't impervious to a bullet."

"Aren't you always saying that you're
about as sensitive and soft as a ton of iron?

I just wish you didn't have to come home hurt, but it is good to have you here, little brother." The look in her eyes said a whole lot more.

He didn't know what to say. He loved his sisters, but he didn't feel comfortable saying so. He didn't feel comfortable with a lot of things.

Amy brought his pancake platter, stacked high with an egg, hash browns and sausage links. His stomach growled. This morning's swim had honed his appetite, so he bowed his head for grace and then grabbed the syrup, content to eat so he wouldn't have to talk.

But his sisters hovered over him, keeping a close eye to whatever he needed. A few diners, friends of the family, stopped to say hello. Some had loved ones in the Middle East. Some just wanted to say they were glad he was home safely.

It should have been nice. It *was* nice. But he was no hero. Just a man who did his job…and hadn't done it well enough. His leg ached, his future stretched out ahead of him like a big bleak question mark and worst of all, he couldn't forget Cadence.

Seeing her again had opened up too many doors in his heart and in his past. It took all his effort to close them tight. He was happy for her and her gold medals. Her fame and glory. Her achievement in her life. He hoped she had everything she wanted. She was a good person and she deserved her success.

The food seemed tasteless, but he kept on eating. He battled to bury the past, and took the local paper Amy offered him on her way down the aisle. The past was over and done with. There wasn't a power anywhere that could change it.

So why did his thoughts keep returning to his morning swim and the woman on guard duty? He'd watched her dive to near perfection over and over again on the grainy little set in the dorm on base. She'd moved like a ballerina, twisted like a gymnast and competed with the poise of a confident, world-class athlete.

He'd watched later as her lovely face, the one he knew so well he could draw it from memory, had filled the TV screen. Tears had shone on her face when she'd sung the national anthem, a gold disk around her neck.

You got what you wanted, he'd thought. He'd stopped watching after her first medal, on the ten-meter platform.

All this time, he'd done his level best not to think of her. He'd been fiercely in love with her once, when he wasn't good enough to kiss the ground at her feet. He'd been nothing but trouble back then, a disaster waiting to happen, and he knew it. Pushing her away then had been the right decision.

She'd gone on to glory and dreams, and he'd found his niche in life, carrying an M-203 and fast roping from helicopters. It was for the best. And that's the way it would stay.

"Ben?" Amy caught his attention, holding on to a tall man. "I want you to meet my fiancé, Heath Murdock. I know you two are going to really get along."

Ben blinked. He took in his baby sister's beaming smile, how she lit up inside when she looked at the quiet man, who had a spine-straight, feet-braced-apart stance that shouted "military." So this was Heath? Reserving judgment, Ben wondered how any man on this planet could be good enough for Amy.

She seemed oblivious to the dark frown he was giving both her and her betrothed, and kept talking. "Heath used to be in the marines."

"Once a marine, always a marine," the stoic stranger commented. He held out his hand. "Good to meet you, Ben."

"You, too." And if you hurt my sister, I'll make you sorry. He couldn't help being protective. Lord knew he hadn't been around when Amy had really needed him before, when her life had taken a painful turn. He shook Heath's hand, liking the fact that he had a solid shake and a good hard stare. Only time would tell about this stranger.

Amy seemed to be pretty sure, judging by the adoration that seemed to radiate from her. She couldn't seem to take her eyes from Heath. The front door opened, a gust of hot wind swept in and she went to greet the newcomers, but her gaze kept returning to the man in the aisle.

Ben recognized the sweetness of Rachel's voice and then the pounding footsteps of a little boy run-walking down the aisle.

Amy's son shouted, "Uncle Ben! Uncle Ben!"

Amy called out, reminding him to walk.

Ben's throat filled. The last time he'd been home, Westin had been a little guy. Here he was, bigger and older and with the long-limbed energy of a seven-year-old. His cowlick stuck straight up, and he was out of breath, wheezing a little. The boy had inherited Ben's childhood asthma, but he looked as if he was doing well.

"Uncle Ben! Are you comin' to my game? I'm gonna hit the ball and everything!"

"Uh, sure, buddy."

Time. It was changing this place and these people. His sisters were older. His nephew was older. Regret tugged hard in his chest, leaving Ben unable to speak as his nephew climbed onto the bench seat on the other side of the booth.

His heart gave a little twist. The tyke looked so much like Ben at that age it was like staring at the little boy he'd been before his parents' car crash. Before his world had fractured into a zillion pieces, never to be made right again.

It still wasn't right. His appetite gone, he shoved the plate aside and opted for the full cup of coffee. Across the table, Westin rocked back and forth, barely containing boyish energy.

For Ben, the memory of his childhood broke apart and time fell back into sync again. He heard pots clatter from the direction of the kitchen. The *ca-ching* of the old cash register. The busy chatter of voices as families gathered together for a Saturday-morning meal.

He was the only one who hadn't changed. The only one who'd remained the same. It was as if life were passing by and he hadn't been part of it.

And never would be.

The coffee tasted acrid on his tongue, even after he added more sugar. Then again, maybe that was just life, bitter instead of sweet.

"Do I have to drag you outta here?" Peggy Jennings called from the office door, her voice echoing in the near silence of the lapping pool waters. "I mean it. I've got a rope."

"Sure you do." Cadence ignored her friend and mentor to concentrate on the teenage girl perched on the edge of the springboard.

Ashley Higgs was a swim team member with hopes of a college scholarship in athletics—not easy to get for those sports outside the big three of football, basketball and baseball.

Since Cadence knew what it was like to work so hard and hope so earnestly, she ended the hour-long session as she always did. "This is the last dive of the day. We worked on some hard stuff, but this one is for fun. Just enjoy."

Ashley huffed a breath, lost in concentration. Fun wasn't so easy. Cadence knew about that, too. Not when everything seemed to be at stake. She backed down the deck, keeping one eye on the girl as she went. The farther away she was, the more likely the student would dive for the love of it. For the sheer joy.

Not today, apparently. Tired from her hard work, Ashley sprang from the board. Once airborne, she wobbled a little too much, didn't keep arch in her back and hit the water with a splash that sent droplets onto the deck. Ashley broke the surface and flew up the ladder, shaking her head, going over in her mind everything that was wrong with that dive.

"Is your family going up to your lake cabin for the rest of the weekend?" Cadence waited, trying to distract the girl. For there was more to life than finding fault with a less than perfect dive, and more to life than diving.

"Yeah. Dad brought the boat up last weekend and wants to go on this lame boat ride." Ashley, the teenager she was, rolled her eyes. "But I'm gonna stay and work on my dives. My uncle cleared beneath the dock—there were some rocks and stuff— and so now it's safe to dive. I'm gonna practice until I can do a back dive pike as perfect as you did in the Olympics, Cadence."

"That was one dive that was right at just the right moment. Besides, in a few years you'll be off at college and away from home all the time. You might want to think about that lame boat ride. You can have fun and still find time to practice, you know."

Ashley rolled her eyes again in that way teenagers had of saying "I know." "Thanks for everything and stuff. I'll have that dive nailed by Monday. I promise!" Ashley hurried off, snagged the towel from the bench and slipped past Peggy at the door.

Peggy's huge key ring jangled. "Hurry. We're gonna be late for the game, and you heard me promise to drag our star pitcher to the field on time."

"Do we have a game today?" Cadence bit the side of her mouth to keep from smiling and watched as Peggy's jaw dropped.

"How could you forget? This is the big game. Against those uptown city pool girls. The ones who trounced us last year because you forgot about the game." Peggy locked the door behind them and followed Cadence through the dim office. "You didn't really forget, did you? Not this time. Not with our relief pitcher in San Diego on vacation."

"I didn't forget." Cadence checked the lockers and the cabinets. She then stole her things from the top of a file cabinet and locked the private office up tight. "And I'm not officially late. Yet. Can we get to the field in four minutes and forty-two seconds?"

"No sweat, but you have to let me fix your hair. You aren't gonna attract a nice, decent man with your hair looking like a gopher's taken up residence in it."

"My hair isn't that bad." Bad-hair days were an occupational hazard of working at a swimming pool. Between lessons and swim team and private lessons and guard duty, there wasn't much of a chance to comb out wet hair after every dunking.

She waited for Peggy to pass through the outer office door, and they finished their routine of locking and setting alarms and waiting for Ashley to finish changing and leave. Hurrying out into the parking lot, Cadence caught her reflection in her sedan's windshield.

Nope, definitely not the best hair day, she thought as she wrestled with her door lock. When the stubborn door opened, she tossed her bag onto the backseat.

Still, she thought on the drive over, it wasn't as if she was going to catch a husband on the baseball diamond in an all-women league. After so much time being single, she wasn't sure she wanted to risk her heart again. Her attempts at romance had ended disastrously—both of them.

I'm happy alone, she decided with absolute certainty as she slipped into one of the last available parking spots along the street. Peggy meant well, but she'd been happily married for over thirty-five years. Not everyone fell in love with their high school sweetheart, married and lived happily ever after.

And speaking of her high school sweetheart, there he was. Down on his knees, Ben McKaslin looked like everything good and decent and awesome in a man as he talked with a little boy somewhere around six or seven. The child was his spitting image. From the high cheekbones and straight blade of a nose to his full mouth to the small dimple cut into a rock-hard chin. Ben's son? He had to be.

The little boy's face had yet to find the hard-edged look that Ben's had, but he was going to grow up as handsome as his dad. The shock of seeing them together made her glad she couldn't be seen.

Somehow in all these years she'd never pictured Ben settling down, marrying a nice woman and raising children.

But he had. Maybe he'd found the best in himself after all.

"Cadence! Over this way!" Across the street and down a way, there was Peggy with her hand over her eyes to shade them, cracking gum and motioning in the opposite direction on the city of Bozeman's huge, multipurpose park.

The baseball diamonds seemed to wink beneath the full force of the afternoon sun, but it was simply the sunlight reflecting off the chain link barrier fencing. The crack of a ball against a bat, the rising cheers, the groan of agony as a runner was called out mixed with the wonderful sounds of the busy ballpark. These reminded Cadence, as always, of why she was here—friends, the love of sports. What better way was there to spend an afternoon?

She glanced over her shoulder to see Ben McKaslin with his son on his shoulders. Cute as a button and alight with happiness, the boy held on tight to the top of Ben's head.

Good. She was glad for him. But a hard sword of hurt sliced her through the midsection. The past and what could have been was right there. Once she'd dreamed of being Ben's wife. Of being happy together. Of holding their baby son in her arms.

It was never your future, she reminded herself. If it had been, then God would have made it possible. The dream of a happy life with Ben had been simply her wish. Another one that had fallen like a star to the earth, incinerating as it fell.

"Hurry! The game's gonna start, and you haven't warmed up that arm of yours," Peggy said, grabbing her by the elbow.

Somehow Cadence moved forward, one foot in front of the other. It was as if too many dreams had burned up. She found it hard to walk through the families milling around or cheering on their loved ones playing in a game. Of all the roads not taken and of all the paths God had decided were not for her, this was the most arduous one.

Loneliness filled her, but it wasn't truly loneliness at all. It was emptiness in her heart where she'd stored up all her love for a husband and family one day.

When it went too long unused, love must disappear as surely as dreams, leaving nothing in its place.

Chapter Five

"Uncle Ben, did you see how far I hit the ball?" Westin skipped, leading the way through the busy maze of T-ball games and the clusters of spectators that went along with each game. "It went *way* far. And fast. Like the speed of light."

Ben laughed. "I saw it, buddy. You did great."

"I know." Westin skipped just a few steps ahead, tossing a softball up in the air and catching it.

Overconfident little tyke, Ben thought, unable to keep from caring about the kid a little bit more.

"You're great with him," Rachel commented from his side. "Being with him makes you want one, doesn't it?"

"Not really." Liar, his conscience mocked him. But that was his story and he was sticking to it. "It's hard to do your job and know your family's waiting at home— while you're deployed most of the year— waiting to be informed of your death."

"You've managed to stay alive all this time." Rachel rolled her eyes, as if she wasn't fooled one bit. "I just think you'd make a great dad if you ever let yourself get close to a nice woman and marry her. You have a good heart."

"If I ever find anyone as sweet and as good as you, Rache, then I swear I'll marry her on the spot. You're the reason I haven't gotten married. It's your fault I'm still single."

"How is it my fault?"

"Because who could ever measure up to you?"

"There was somebody once—" Rachel turned to grab Westin's softball. "You're gonna clunk into someone if you're not careful."

"Hey! No fair." Westin stopped and

planted both hands on his hips. His indignation was cute, and he knew it. "Can I have my ball? Please?"

"No." Rachel stood her ground. "You'll get it back when there's no one around for you to accidentally hit."

Ben grabbed the softball from her hand, and she hadn't even seen it coming. One moment she was gently scolding their nephew and the next she was staring at him with openmouthed accusation.

"You are in hot water, too, mister." Rachel could pretend to be scolding all she wanted, but neither of them was fooled. She was a big softy, and he could charm her out of any mood. "Ben McKaslin, give me that ball."

"Nope." He tugged on her ponytail instead, and watched a flush rise in her face. "Ah, I haven't tormented you for way too long—"

"Look out!" someone shouted from behind him, but it was too late.

He knew he was in trouble, as if an angel nudged at his shoulder, but he was already stepping toward Rachel to give her ponytail another tug. Something hit the back of his head so hard, his vision blurred, stars exploded in front of his eyes and he dropped to his knees.

Some sisters might have commented that he'd gotten what he deserved, but not Rachel. She was on her knees beside him, with a newly caught softball in her hand and brushing at his face with the other. "Are you all right? Ben? Can you hear me?"

"Uh, sure."

"Are you okay?"

"Yes, okay." Pain dizzied him. His stomach rolled, but everything stayed down. He pushed a hand against the ground so he wouldn't embarrass himself further by falling over. He had no idea where his crutches were. Only that his head hurt as if someone had tried to crack it open.

"I'm so sorry." A woman's voice came from somewhere behind him. A woman's familiar voice.

If his head would stop spinning and pounding maybe he could place who the woman was. All he could do was moan and push away Rachel's offer of a paper cup full of ice. Other voices around him blurred and melded into one huge background noise. The sunlight became stabbing.

Then he gazed upward and his hazy vision blurred on a woman's form, her sleek dark hair and her heart-shaped face very familiar.

The harsh midafternoon sun blazed downward, blinding him, and the pain of the light was like a physical blow. Air whooshed out of his lungs as if he'd been sucker punched. But in that strange airless state his eyes cleared and it was Cadence he saw, hovering over him, concern soft upon her dear face. It was her voice that he heard above all others, when so many people were talking at once.

"Ben. Are you all right?" she asked softly.

No, he wasn't all right, because he was imagining her again. It had to be a concussion, he figured, or worse. What other reason could there be that he'd imagined the only woman he'd ever loved?

Only a strange misfiring of neurons, since God wouldn't be that cruel as to bring him face-to-face with Cadence

Chapman one more time. To show him everything he could never have. It was like showing heaven to a condemned soul. For one millisecond he hoped she really was there, and then he tasted the bitter reality. The air rushed back into his lungs and his sight returned. She was not there, hovering before him like a dream.

"I'm fine, really," he told his hovering sisters, who'd caught up with them and were getting ready to diagnose a concussion. "I have a really hard head, so I'm fine. I've taken worse blows before this."

"That explains a lot," the voice that was so like Cadence's commented dryly as she pressed a paper cup of ice to his head. "Feel better?"

"Heaps."

Cadence? It was her? He watched as she knelt beside him, lithe and graceful as a ballerina, as wholesome as the girl next door, and real flesh and blood. No dream. No figment of his imagination.

What are you doing here? he wondered, but didn't ask. He could only stare in amazement as she leaned to inspect the back of his head. She smelled like those purple flowers his mom would always plant in the flower beds right up close to the house. It was a soothing scent. Lavender, that's what it was, and the scent suited her, he thought as her fingertips grazed the back of his head.

"Oh, you already have a lump there. I think you need to go to the hospital and have a doctor look at that."

"I don't have a concussion. Did you have to be the one to hit me in the head with a ball?" He wanted to be annoyed with her.

The pain in his head was beyond annoying, but Cadence could never be. Concern softened her lovely features as she knelt close to study the size of his pupils. He hated how having her so close tugged at something within him. Like a long-forgotten door in his heart. A door he'd locked on purpose. "I've survived gunfire and grenades and explosives. A baseball is nothing."

"Oh." As if he'd slapped her, she jerked away. "I see. I guess you're just fine. Good. It was nice seeing you, too."

She rose to her full height, and from his

position flat on the ground she appeared taller than her petite five-three. Her dark hair whipped around her shoulders, the ends of the ponytail lashing back and forth, and she looked like an Amazon out for vengeance. Except her face wasn't fierce looking, but pitying.

Pitying. What? As if he'd turned out so bad after all? Or what? Then again, maybe it wasn't pity he was reading on her face. It was certainly something else as she dismissed him and looked over her right shoulder.

"Are you gonna hafta go into the hospital, too?" Westin had gone ashen pale as he clutched Amy's hand, snuggling up against her legs like a frightened puppy. "They got grape Popsicles there."

The boy's words were meant to be encouraging, but Ben's chest cracked with pain. Amy had written about the incident earlier in the summer when Westin had nearly drowned in the river. "Thanks, buddy. I'm okay. Don't you worry about me, got it?"

Westin's wide eyes remained owlish, but he nodded. "Okay, Uncle Ben. If you gotta go, me and Mom could stay with you. So you don't get scared."

Amy knelt to draw the boy into her arms. "That's mighty brave of you, but Uncle Ben's going to be all right. We'll get some pizza and that'll fix him right up. What do you say, Ben?"

"Sure. Pizza is a respected cure for headache pain."

Cadence felt the earth shift beneath her feet. The boy was Amy's son? Not Ben's? Her brain screeched to a halt as she watched the McKaslin clan—people she hadn't seen since high school—gather around Ben. He rose to his feet and his family handed him his crutches, concerned but hiding it behind gentle kidding comments meant to make him smile.

Ben took his crutches casually, as if they were no big deal at all, and that's when she noticed the surgical scars running up the length of his calf. And the unmistakable red-purplish round scar, about the size of a quarter, that could be only one thing—a bullet wound. He'd been injured in the line of duty. Wounded defending their country.

Respect hit her square in the chest, as if

she'd been the one to take a wayward fast-ball. The brightness of the sun, the motion and activity on the fields surrounding them, the noise of the games and the scent of summer on the wind faded into nothing.

Only Ben filled the center of her senses—how he positioned the crutches and leaned on them, saying God had graced him with a hard head for a reason, reassuring Paige that he was telling the truth.

Then he turned to wink at her, as if to let her know there were no hard feelings. The breeze puffed through his short dark hair and brought her the scent of his aftershave, woodsy and crisp—the same, after all these years.

This was the man who'd abandoned her first. The one who'd said he'd never settle down. He wasn't made to be held back. He was meant for bigger and better things than being tied down to a wife and a diner the way his dad was.

It was hard not to let the anger rise, even after all these years. She'd thought she'd found peace, that she'd moved past an event that had happened almost half a lifetime ago. She'd been wrong. Forgiveness had many layers. It was hard to take a step back from the family she'd once known so well. Paige was in her late thirties now; the last time Paige had spoken to her, she'd been a young wife with a baby on her arm. The strapping teenage boy standing next to her had to be that baby son.

And Rachel and Amy had been high school and junior high girls. Cadence wondered how so much time could slip away when she wasn't looking.

Amy took her son by the hand, and a ring sparkled on her fourth finger. Marriages and children and family—those were the things that mattered. That gave each year more precious meaning than the last.

Before the family's conversation could turn to her—they'd established that Ben was fine and Westin, who'd been hospitalized apparently, was no longer worried for his uncle's welfare—she took another step back. Her teammates were calling for her and it would be so easy to step back into the crowd and disappear without saying another word to the McKaslins.

The busyness and noise of the city's huge baseball park returned and she waved to Rachel, who appeared to be the only one noticing her departure.

An arm clasped her shoulders. It was Paige. "The last time I saw you, you were on TV wearing a shiny medal."

When Cadence studied Paige's face, she saw there was only kindness reflected in her brown eyes, and the tension inside her eased. Whatever hard feelings there had been long ago when she and Ben broke up were not here today. Some things in the past were truly forgiven, and for that Cadence was thankful. She'd so loved Ben's sisters and, judging from the rush of affection within her, that was something that hadn't changed either. "I was very blessed during that time in my life. How are you?"

"Surviving. This is only my second T-ball game since my boy was little, and things were different then. There were no fancy parks like this for the kids. You play on a team. How come we didn't see you last week?"

"I was out of town."

"I hear rumors about you now and then.

Traveling to events and competitions. You're doing something with the college?"

"I'm adjunct to the sports departments. I coach, since a lot of kids on the university teams used to be mine through high school."

"Was that why you were out of town?"

"No, I went to visit a friend this time. Tell me—"

Paige was ready with another question. "A friend? I notice there's no wedding ring on your finger. Does that mean you're still looking for the right guy? Or is this friend the one?"

Was Paige fishing for information, Cadence wondered, or was she simply asking out of courtesy? "No, this is a Romanian diver I met when I was competing. Olga and I struck up a friendship."

"Is she the one who was supposed to be your big rival?"

"There was no rivalry, although I think the media tried to put that spin on it. Diving isn't the most exciting Olympic sport. It's pretty peaceful, so I imagine that rumor spiced things up a bit during the coverage. But Olga and I have always had the greatest respect for one another. She's coaching in Australia now, and I had gone down to see her during the Sydney Games…it's a long story. Anyway, we've always kept in touch. She is a true friend." One who'd stuck with her through thick and thin.

"And a great blessing." Paige seemed to study her, as if she could see past the layers to the truth beneath. "I can't imagine your life could have been easy then, as beautifully as you dove. It must be a great relief to be back home in Montana."

"It's where I want to be."

"Then stop by the diner sometime when you're driving through town to see your mom. You can have a chocolate shake for old times' sake. And come and visit with me, all right?"

A sincere invitation. After all she'd been through, Cadence appreciated it. She'd learned the hard way what was truly important. "I'd like that."

"Good. Now, you have to come to Amy's wedding."

"Oh, absolutely." Amy joined them. "The wedding is next month, and I'd love for you to come. I didn't know you were living back home."

"I have a place here in Bozeman."

"Then give me your address and I'll send an invitation."

Amy had grown up to be such a lovely woman, Cadence thought as she waited while the sisters began digging in their purses for pen and paper.

"When I think of you, I remember a ten-year-old girl with pigtails," Cadence confessed. "It's hard to believe you're a mom."

"Westin just turned seven." Amy pulled a pen from the depths of her purse, while Rachel crowded in with a small notebook from her book bag.

Cadence gave the required information, aware that the softball game was continuing without her and that Ben had deliberately stepped aside with Amy's son. Of all the people that ball could have hit, did it have to be him? He seemed to have recovered and perhaps felt uncomfortable, the same way she did, since he'd turned his back to her.

Since she didn't believe in coincidence, she had to wonder why Ben McKaslin kept crossing her path. What was God trying to tell her?

"Did you know that Cadence isn't married?" Paige seemed to be speaking with her sisters, but a sparkle glinted in her eyes as she met Cadence's gaze. "Still single after all these years."

"No, really?" Rachel leaned closer, greatly interested. "How strange, because Ben isn't married either."

"A coincidence. Some might say that was a sign from above," Amy added.

No way. Cadence knew exactly where this was going. "I haven't met the right man at just the right time. I'm in no hurry."

"Love happens when it happens," Amy said sagely, radiating happiness, the diamond engagement ring sparkling on her left hand. "It's even sweeter the second time around."

Pain cracked like a broken rib in her chest, and Cadence spoke before the well-meaning sisters could take this one step further. "I'm not interested in getting married. I figure if it hasn't happened yet, it probably won't. I love my life exactly the way it is. Although I'm happy for you, Amy."

"Come have pizza with us," Paige invited, speaking over her sister. "When your game's done, just come on over. We're going to the restaurant just on the other side of the park. I'm told everyone goes there after their games."

"No." Her gaze shot past Paige's shoulder. "This is your family time."

"You're like family," Rachel piped up. "At least stop by so we can catch up. We can be friends like we used to be."

Cadence's chest cracked a little more. After all she'd been through, how could she say no to that? "I'll stop by, if I can find you. The restaurant gets packed."

"Good enough." Paige beamed with approval. She was a beautiful woman with a gentle smile that seemed to be reassuring.

Cadence could feel the wings of disaster fluttering overhead. "I've got to get back. It was good seeing you all."

As their cheerful and rather hopeful-sounding goodbyes rang in the air behind her, she spun on her cleats and ran back to her game. Hurt welled up over the what-ifs in her life, the places where so many times the forks in her path could have brought her marriage and family and hadn't.

Her team was up, and she weaved through the spectators toward the barrier fence behind home plate. She felt Ben's gaze on her all the while, like a lasso wrapping tight around her throat as if to haul her back. But she was stronger than that and kept on going. She took her place in line with her team.

"Lucky that guy wasn't hurt much," Peggy commented. "People have really gotten hurt that way."

Cadence nodded, focusing on the opposing team as their pitcher wound up—she had a killer slow-pitch. She kept her thoughts on the game where they belonged, because as much as she'd once loved the McKaslin girls, they hadn't become her family. As much as she'd loved Ben, he had never loved her the same in return.

So much time had passed and so much life had happened to both of them that now Ben McKaslin was just some guy to her. It was all he would ever be.

As if an angel touched her on the shoulder, she turned to the exact position where she could see the McKaslin family meandering through the busy park, talking amicably the way a family should. The little boy skipped ahead, followed by Ben on his crutches, the metal glinting sharply in the sun as he moved. His strong arm muscles bunched and rippled as he went.

With any luck, the restaurant would be too crowded and there would no need to see him again. And if she did, there was no reason to think things could be any different this time. Life wasn't like that.

She'd learned that the hard way, too.

Chapter Six

Why did his gaze find her the instant she strolled into the restaurant? Ben wondered. Especially when he'd intentionally chosen a table as far away from the front door as he could get and sat with his back to the front of the restaurant?

"See? You're drawn to her." Rachel leaned to speak into his ear. "Somebody better go over and invite her to sit with us. If he doesn't, then one of his sisters will."

"Stay out of this, please." He said it firmly so she understood. But he didn't want to hurt her feelings, and took her hand. Rachel was such a sweetie it was impossible not to take care with her. "I appreciate what you're doing, but it's not what I want, pretty lady."

"I think you're making a terrible mistake. She looks sad, don't you think?"

Her question made him turn and look again at the petite wisp of a woman with her dark hair swept up in a ponytail, wearing her team's jersey and shorts.

No. She didn't look sad. Not one bit. She was laughing and talking with other women from her team. Her smile was wide, and from this angle he could see only a three-quarter view of her face, but she looked happy enough. Then again, how could one really know that about another person from just a glance?

"Can you imagine why she hasn't gotten married? Not in all this time?"

"Did you not hear me?"

"Oh, I hear you, brother dear. I just feel a calling, if you know what I mean. As if this moment is so much bigger. I think heaven has brought you two back together for a reason."

Ben rolled his eyes. "Back together? We're not back together. We've bumped into one another. And you aren't helping things at all. Do not call her over here."

"It won't matter if you threaten or not. If it's meant to be, it's meant to be."

"I'm going to get some pizza. I know you mean well, but this is only going to wind up hurting me. I'm here only for a while. I'm going back to active duty as soon as I can, and my work is on the other side of the globe. See?"

"Yeah, I do." Rachel didn't look too disappointed as she dug her fork into her heaping plate of salad. "Look, they've just put up more pizza. Go get me some pepperoni, would you?"

"As long as you promise to sit still—and don't you contact Cadence in any way. Not through Amy or Paige. Don't use Westin. You're sneaky."

"I am a sneaky one." She didn't look guilty in the least.

"Can I trust you?"

"Implicitly." With a coy smirk she lifted her fork in the air. "Go on. Bring some for Paige, too. Paige, do you want more pizza?"

He knew as well as Rachel did that

Paige would answer in the affirmative. And so he grabbed his crutches and accepted Westin's offer to help carry the plates. The two of them made their way to the buffet by skirting around tables and groups of people and kids running toward the video games.

"Here's the pepperoni, Uncle Ben!" Westin surged ahead and politely got into line behind a petite woman in a blue-and-white shirt and shorts and with a silky black ponytail sweeping her shoulder blades.

So Rachel had noticed Cadence was going toward the pizza buffet, had she? Well, there was no need to hide. He could handle this and show his sisters that they were wrong. And he'd show himself that Cadence Chapman didn't affect him. That he was big enough to leave the past where it belonged. They were both older now. Wiser. Hopefully a little more compassionate.

"Hey, Cadence." He sidled up to the buffet next to her. "How did your game turn out?"

She didn't seem at all surprised to see

him, which told him she'd probably spotted him earlier, too. She slid a slice of pepperoni onto her plate and inched down to the vegetarian pizza. "We won by three runs. How's your head?"

"Fine. Good. Hardly a bump. What were the odds?"

"Astronomical, but that shouldn't surprise me. Life throws a lot of curves at a person."

"Or hits him in the head," Ben quipped.

"Exactly." A smile stretched across her face, not as wide and unrestrained as her smile used to be.

Up this close, he saw a lot of changes on her face. Hers was no longer soft as a teenager's, youthful and unmarked. Time had made its presence known, had tucked character into the corners of her eyes and brackets at the corners of her mouth. Somehow the change was an improvement. But what he could not miss was the wariness in her eyes.

He hadn't put that there, had he? "My sisters sure want you to come join us. I wouldn't mind it much either."

"Not much?"

"I'm getting used to looking the past in the face. It isn't easy, but it's my own fault. I made mistakes that can't be undone."

"Me, too. We're blocking others from getting their pizza."

"Yeah, Uncle Ben," Westin agreed, and led the way toward the table.

Ben hesitated. "If you're busy with your friends, I get that. You must do this every Saturday."

"Something like that." Cadence held back her emotions. Maybe she and Ben had something in common after all. He'd spoken of mistakes and regrets. She knew something about those things. "I'd like to come over as soon as I get something to eat. I'm starving."

"You might as well visit us and eat at the same time. You can get it over with and then get back to your friends." He winked, still charming after all these years.

"You make it sound as if talking to your sisters is something to dread." She couldn't help but smile, because there was no missing the fondness Ben had for his sisters.

"If I bring you over, they'll think it was my doing and they'll be nicer to me. You know how mean my sisters are to me."

"Yes, I do. It's a pity, really, how they treat you."

The dimple cut into his cheek, and he must have known there was no way she could refuse that charming dimple. Or the man who made it. After all these years she'd gotten good at saying no. She'd had to learn that the hard way. But apparently there was still one person she wouldn't say no to. And he had the feel of disaster to him. Not in his all-American good looks or in his dependable calmness that made her think the rebellious teenager had grown into a responsible man. That was the danger—look how wonderful he'd become. Her heart twisted with hurt.

Hurt—that's all the young Ben McKaslin had ever been able to do. She wasn't so sure she ought to trust the older, improved version.

She took a step along with him, wondering what she was doing. Bantering with him as if it were old times. Going along with his suggestion. Acting as if the past didn't remain a sore between them. What was she thinking? Ben McKaslin hadn't changed one bit. She'd hoped he'd married and found happiness, but he'd never settled down. Even if he was here to stay, it didn't matter. She wanted nothing to do romantically with a man who had a proven track record at leaving. Lord knows she'd been through that enough in her life.

The little boy cleared the way, rounding tables and weaving a path to the long table in the back, where large windows faced the busy ballpark and cast brightness over the family seated there. Paige and her son. Amy and Rachel. And one empty chair, as if they'd been waiting for her.

Amy spotted her first, broke away from the conversation and her eyes lit with genuine warmth. "Cadence. I'm so glad you took us up on our offer. Come talk to us. I have a place saved for you right here."

Right next to a chair where a soda glass stood with a straw in it beside a wadded-up napkin. She didn't need to ask who was sitting in that spot. And she wasn't surprised at all when Ben set his pizza plate there. The sisters were matchmaking a little, were they?

She tried to forgive them for it, for they meant well. "I'm here with my team, but I wanted to stop by. You were always family to me, and I've been living here for about two years, but I never seem to run across anyone from my high school days anymore. So many people have moved into the Bozeman area, it's incredible."

"We're growing out our way, too. Manhattan, Montana, is still a one-main-street town, but we have more businesses and the downtown area is regenerating. So many commuters are moving out to buy more affordable housing."

"Which just drives up the price for the rest of us." Amy shrugged. "Heath and I have been house hunting. There's no way the three of us will fit comfortably in my little trailer, but we can't find anything we can both afford and like."

"That's why I'm renting." Casual conversation. Small talk. Cadence resigned herself to it as she set her plate on the table. This is what happened when bonds of friendships dissolved. It was strange how lives intersected for a while, and then parted. Like cars meeting on the freeway, driving parallel for some time, before continuing along on separate paths.

"Allow me." Ben's deep baritone drew her away from her thoughts. He was so close, she could feel the warm fan of his breath against the back of her neck as he leaned to pull out her chair.

"Thank you." She hadn't expected courtesy. Her heart wrenched and she settled onto the hard plastic chair, hardly aware of how uncomfortable it was or the fact that his entire family was staring at them. Old longings rose to the surface. Not for the teenage boy Ben used to be, but for the man she'd always wished he could be. That he would be. For her.

Ben withdrew, and it was as if he took the sunlight with him. All the warmth in the room and all the sparkling brightness seemed to leave, too. She sat in half shadows and, shivering, tried to clear the emotion from her throat and make her heart stop hurting. She whispered a brief prayer.

"So, Cadence." Rachel was all not-so-innocent interest. "Now, what is it that you do for a living?"

Apparently Ben hadn't told them he'd seen her at his recent lap swim. He appeared equally innocent as he took a ravenous bite of pepperoni pizza. With his sisters so interested in matching him up, she certainly understood why. "I teach swimming at the county pool next door."

"Swimming?" Amy perked up. "Are lessons pretty expensive?"

"No." Cadence's gaze shot to Amy's son, who was industriously pulling the pepperoni pieces off his slice, eating one and then taking a bite of pizza. "We have group lessons and, believe me, they are very affordable."

"Really?"

"Yeah. Your son is the right age. We just started a new session of lessons this week. It's not too late to start. Do you want to get him in Monday?"

"If I can make payments and if his uncle can ferry him, then absolutely. After he nearly drowned—oh, it still makes me shake—I have been thinking about teaching him to swim. This seems heaven-sent."

"He got swept away by the river," Rachel explained. "We were all pretty scared about this little guy, but he came through all right."

"My new dad saved me. Well, he ain't

my new dad yet, but he's gonna be." Westin stared hard at Cadence over the top of the table. "I'm not gettin' into that river."

"Have you ever been in a pool?"

"I have one at home. It's big enough to sit in." He tore another pepperoni slice from his pie and popped it into his mouth.

"I bet my pool is bigger than yours. Come see me on Monday and I'll show you. Amy, the beginner class is at eleven-thirty. Have him in his suit and on deck by then, and I'll take especially good care of him."

"Oh, I would be so grateful." Gratitude shone in Amy's eyes. And relief.

Perhaps that is why God brought me here, Cadence thought. To help Amy's son. Purpose lit her up and suddenly the past no longer mattered. Or her regrets or her longings or her dreams, which had faded into nothing.

"I've got to get back to my team," she explained, standing and taking her tray with her. "But it was lovely seeing all of you again. You know where I am, so you don't have to be a stranger."

"Likewise, Cadence," Paige called out.

She didn't dare look at Ben as she walked away, feeling the importance of being one life that belonged to God. Knowing she was fulfilling His plan for her life. She wasn't saving the world like Ben, but she taught children to swim. Sure, she coached and helped divers and swimmers to reach their potential. But diving was a passion, not her calling. Teaching was. And it made a difference.

More certain of her path than she'd been in a long time, she made her way through the restaurant and didn't look back.

After waving off his family, Ben figured he'd have a long wait. Cadence was still in the restaurant with her friends and teammates. Talking and laughing and talking. And talking.

Out on the field, more ball games had ended and hungry participants jammed the parking lot and trekked into the restaurant. Other parties left, disbanding to climb into their separate vehicles and drive off. But not Cadence's group. On his crutches Ben moved to the edge of the parking lot where the park met pavement and squinted into the shadows cast by the tall trees. He watched a men's game in progress.

He'd never been much of a baseball fan. Give him football and hockey any day. But he found himself caught up in the game, wishing he had better use of his leg. Remembering the games some of the guys would play in their two minutes of leisure time.

He wondered about the men playing on the field in front of him, obviously husbands and fathers, judging by the number of women and children watching.

Would he have been one of them if his life had turned out differently? If he'd married Cadence the way everybody thought he should, settled down, made mortgage payments and raised a couple of kids?

No, his life would never have been that neat and tidy. He was called to be a soldier, there was no doubt about that. And Cadence had been destined for gold—something she would have had to give up to be a wife and mother. At least, in Nowhere, Montana, where the nearest training facility was…well, he didn't know where, but it was a long way from here.

The restaurant door opened, and a soft lilt of laughter had him turning, his soul recognizing Cadence before his mind could. She was leaving with four other women of varying ages. The instant his gaze found her, she looked up. Their eyes met. Awareness shot through his chest.

"I'll see you Monday morning bright and early," Cadence said to her friends, and then she headed toward him, sleek and athletically graceful, as always. She was still wearing her baseball cleats, white socks and uniform, and in a flash he remembered Cadence on the high school's softball team, pitching them all the way to state, where they came in second.

She was no longer fresh faced and so unbearably young, yet he saw something of the past in the wise, centered woman. It lingered in both of them, and he could still feel the rapid flutter of her heartbeat as if it were his own. He could feel her wonder and her worry at seeing him.

She hesitated, pausing and then stepping toward him. "Did your sisters head home?"

He nodded. "Paige and Rachel have the

evening shift at the diner, and Amy has plans with the dude she's gonna marry."

"You don't like her choice?"

"Heath seems like an all-right guy and he treats her real nice, but she's my sister. Who could ever be good enough?"

"Point taken. I suppose you and I are going to be seeing more of each other if your nephew joins my beginners class, which I hope he does."

"Looks like it." He pivoted on his crutches, because this was going to be easier if he didn't have to look at her. He watched the men's game instead, bases loaded and a batter up. "We have unfinished business, you and me. You can feel it. I can feel it."

"True."

"The thing is, I don't want this to be hard when it doesn't have to be. So let me just say this and get it over with. I'm sorry for what I did to you. For walking out on you and making it seem like it was your fault."

"It's over, Ben. I don't need to resurrect it."

"It wasn't your fault, you know. It was me. I'm not a stand-in-the-wings kind of man. We never could have made it, you know. We both would have had to give up our dreams."

She swallowed hard. There was the past, looming up like a movie on an enormous drive-in screen hovering overhead in Technicolor glory. Ben telling her he wasn't made to be tied down. Ben telling her, "I don't want you like that. I don't want this," as he gestured to her parents' house, neat and tidy on the quarter acre, almost identical to the others in the subdivision. "I don't want to marry you. I just don't want…you."

The past still hurt.

"It's all right, Ben," she said tightly. "That happened a long time ago."

"It always ate at me. What I said. It was wrong." He stared down at the toe of his running shoe. "I hurt you."

"You did." She took a shuddery breath and held it, breathing out, wishing the pain within her would go as easily as the pent-up air. "But you did nothing more than be honest with me. You told me the truth. You were honest."

"No, I wasn't. I was scared that I'd fail

you, and so I made sure I ended it before I *could* fail you. Before you stopped looking at me with awe and perfect love for me in your eyes."

He paused, grimacing as if he were in pain. "If I'd stayed and we'd tried to make a relationship, maybe even marriage work, I thought I'd ruin it just like I did everything else. It's stupid, I know that now, but I was eighteen and I was dumb and selfish. I didn't want you ever to look at me with regret in your eyes. The way you're looking at me now."

Oh. That wasn't what she'd expected him to say. He'd wanted her? He'd been afraid of failing her? That didn't make any sense. She couldn't reconcile that with the image of the fiery young man he'd been, so confident and free-spirited. "I'm sorry, too. I've already regretted what I said to you."

"That you didn't want anything to hold you back?"

"It was a knee-jerk reflex. If I had to have chosen, Ben, I would have chosen to be with you."

"That never would have worked. We

both knew it then. There's no reason that either of us should hurt over what couldn't be changed. It's over. Done with. Can we bury the past?"

It was a perfectly reasonable request. It was the right one. Cadence was surprised at the relief that rushed through her. "I'd be grateful if we did."

"Then it's done. You and I start fresh from here. When I show up with Westin, it's a clean slate."

A clean slate. It was smart, it was reasonable and it was the right solution. She could feel it down to her bones. There was no fix for the past and the regret that went hand in hand with it. Yes, it was pointless to hold on to something that had no bearing on the present. "You've matured into quite a man, Ben McKaslin."

"I'm surprised you didn't notice that before." He winked, playing as if he was still the same arrogant and charming teen, but it didn't go over well at all. She saw right through him to the man he was. One of strength and integrity. One who had made something of himself. He'd found the best in himself, after all.

"I'll see you on Monday, Ben." It was easier now to walk away. "Take care of your leg. I hope your head feels better. I really am sorry about the softball."

He didn't say anything. He just waved in acknowledgment. She lost sight of him as she found her car and backed out of a space while several other cars were waiting to vie for it.

On the way out she spotted him again, a lone man standing at the edge of the ballpark with sunset streaking the sky above him. A lone man watching the world around him—families and friends and everyday life.

The image of him alone, a man apart, remained long after she could no longer see him in her rearview mirror. Long into the evening in her cozy little town house. Deep in her dreams through the night.

When she woke with the dawn's light, he was there in her mind. The two of them, his life and her life, each and separately alone.

Chapter Seven

She was *not* watching for Ben to arrive. Really. At least, that's what Cadence told herself at the end of her eleven-o'clock advanced beginners class.

As her students shivered at poolside, waiting their turn to dive in and practice their backstroke, she paced alongside the swimmers and offered helpful comments—with one eye on the bleachers.

Okay, she was watching for him. There was no sense in not being honest with herself. He wanted the past buried. It helped knowing he had the same regrets she did. And the same sense of loss that though she'd loved with all her heart and soul, theirs was a love that could never have worked. If they'd married, how would they have made it? Would they have been a divorce statistic? Or would they have managed to hold tight to their holy vows in a tough world, with nothing but failed hopes and unrequited dreams between them?

Would she have resented him if she'd never had the chance to compete for gold? Would he have resented her and been restless and unhappy being a short order cook in his family's diner for the rest of his life? Probably. They would be like some sad families she saw, moms overworked and overburdened, who'd lost joy in their lives. They came with their children, were fine mothers, had nice kids, but during the lesson and when the lessons were over they were the moms who did not smile and wave at their little ones. Who seemed weighed down by sadness and the stress of their lives. Instead of the ones who found better ways to cope with the tough work of being a wife and mother.

She didn't know. Maybe those sadder women were not sad over lost dreams the way she imagined them to be. She only knew that she could never have been whole unless she'd found out what she could do in life. She'd hoped it would make her a better mom when the time came. Not that it looked as if she would ever get the chance now. *Or will I, Lord?*

As the pair of students reached the far end and climbed out, dripping and breathing hard, she nodded to the next pair standing in line. They dived into the water. One splashed as feet smacked against the surface and the other made a whopping belly flop.

Not the best diving technique. They'd have to work on that later, she decided as she watched the kids roll over. Their faces were scrunched up against the water trying to cover them as they kicked feverishly.

"Arms over your heads," she called, demonstrating. "Reach way back."

One—Andrea—managed to fling her arms back, thereby straightening out her body and popping her right to the surface. The girl began her unpracticed backstroke. "Great, Andrea! Travis? Travis, put your head back in the water."

He looked at her, helplessly folded in

two, his feet at the surface, his arms flailing to keep his face above water.

"You're doing good. Just reach back." She lifted her arms again so he could imitate her, and it seemed to help. He stayed rigid, bent in the middle, but at least he was lying back on the water.

Except he was also submerging. He came up sputtering, treading water.

"That's good. Try it again from the wall. You're getting it. It just takes practice, okay?" She said it kindly, because she knew the other kids were trying not to snicker and failing. She shot them a firm glance, arching one brow to look more imposing. "You may have the same trouble, you know. That's great, Travis. Reach behind you. Don't look at your toes!"

He struggled, but he moved sluggishly across the pool. Andrea had already climbed out and was dripping on the deck.

Ben's here.

She could feel his presence like a touch. Her heart skipped a beat. It was as if the world froze in time for one fraction of a moment as she gazed upward exactly to where he stood in a middle aisle of the half-filled bleachers. She wanted to scold herself for having such a strident reaction to Ben's arrival. Was it old feelings long buried? Or was it because she could look at him and no longer feel the pain of regret?

He caught her gaze and gave her a small, tight salute, the dimples cutting into his cheeks as he slouched down onto an empty bench. He looked away, breaking their connection.

The moment faded, leaving only the present—the call of other instructors' voices on the other side of the pool echoing overhead, the slosh and splish of the water, the rush of kids swimming, the glare of sunlight through the skylights. Travis reached the far end and she congratulated him, then called in the last pair for the last swim of the day.

By the time she made promises for practicing their dives next time and said goodbye, her next class was lined up on the wooden benches along the wall, shivering from their shower. Ben's nephew was among them, lean and spare, looking wide-eyed at the water as if he thought swimming lessons were the worst idea ever.

Remembering how his family had said he'd nearly drowned in the river last month, she didn't blame him one bit. She hopped in to help switch the ropes, dividing the pool widthwise rather than lengthwise. Peggy rolled her eyes in silent misery. She liked teaching the deep end of the pool the least, but Cadence loved it all. Every class, every stage, every student.

Because of the work they did here, the chances of these children drowning in a preventable incident were drastically reduced. She'd never know how many lives she saved by teaching kids to swim and swim well, and it heartened her as she clamped the final rope, ducked beneath it and approached the shallow end of the pool.

Eight little kids stared back at her in various stages of eagerness. From confident Kaylie in her pink ruffle suit and hair in neat little braids, to Jacob with a glint of trouble in his eyes ready for the class to be over, to Westin who'd gone pale when he realized other classes were being called to the water's edge. His class was bound to be next.

Yep, she had her work cut out for her. And she liked it that way. Placing her hands on the deck, she studied her cute little students. "Hey, I'm so jazzed to see you guys again. Did any of you remember to practice like I asked you to?"

Kaylie's hand shot up. "I did! I did! I blowed the biggest bubbles ever!"

"Right." Jacob rocked back to stare at the ceiling, as if he were contemplating shimmying up to the rafters and seeing if the skylights opened—his only chance of escape.

Westin swallowed hard. His hand waved. "Do I hafta put my face in?"

"We're only doing it halfway," she answered. "Don't worry. I promise to help you. Kaylie, do you remember how to use the ladder?"

"Do I!" Eager to be the first one in, the little girl walked importantly the few feet to the access ladder, gripped the big metal rails and backed down into the water. Cadence caught her by the elbow and steadied her while Kaylie gripped the edge of the wall.

"Excellent." Figuring she'd best get Jacob into the pool before he implemented an escape plan, she called him next.

Highly uninterested, he climbed into the water and took his place beside Kaylie. No big deal.

"Don't splash, hotshot," she reminded him as she called her next student, a quiet little girl.

Madison was tentative, but she did a good job. As did the next four students.

She'd left Westin for last, so he could watch the others and see nothing scary had happened to them.

He looked at her with big eyes, so dark and familiar it was like looking at Ben when he was that age. "Do I hafta?" he whispered so only she could hear, while darting glances at the kids already in the water beside her.

"I'll be right here. I won't let you slip, okay?" she reassured him, holding out both hands to help Westin down. "Jacob, no splashing," she called over her shoulder.

"You know my mom and my uncle Ben." Westin nodded as if he were coming to a decision, and gripped the ladder rail with all his might. His entire hand turned white. He shifted weight uncertainly and stretched to find the next step with his right leg.

"You're going great. Just keep coming." She cupped his elbow, gripping him firmly so he wouldn't fall.

Tension quaked in his tensed muscles, and his little arm felt so frail. But like Ben at that age, he was tough. He shifted his weight again, reaching downward to the next step before his toes hit the water.

"See? Almost there."

"This don't grab like the river." A smile brightened his face and the tension eased somewhat.

Victory. Cadence helped him to the edge and made sure he was holding on tight. As soon as he discovered his feet touched the ground and his chin was just out of the water, he relaxed and joined in with the other kids hopping and splashing a little in place.

"Let's see your bubble faces!" she called out. "Everyone show me."

She puffed up her cheeks with air and made sure Westin knew to join in. With only a look he was puffing up, too, like a cute little blowfish, and they practiced blowing bubbles in the air first.

As involved as she became teaching her beginner class, she could never quite forget the tall, lean man in the upper row watching her.

Ben couldn't take it anymore. The big clock on the far wall read 11:50. He'd lasted twenty minutes. He'd given it his best, but he was done.

Another minute of watching Cadence and he was going to break the promise he'd made to himself. No more regrets. No glimpses back at old failures. Which was easy enough to do as long as he wasn't anywhere near Cadence Chapman.

She seemed to be the only person he could see. Every time he deliberately tried to watch Westin nervously lowering his face to blow bubbles on the water's surface or holding tight to the side of the pool and learning to lie out on his stomach and kick until he splashed, Ben's gaze strayed to Cadence. Every time. What was wrong with him? He commanded himself to look away. But his eyes kept finding her no matter what he did, and there seemed to be no willpower strong enough to stop him.

Her dark hair gathered high into a single braided ponytail, she waded between the kids, giving them pointers and encouragement. The blue one-piece she wore was modest, but the color matched her sapphire-blue eyes and the sight of her took his breath away. Her heart-shaped face was softened by the water droplets flung her way as the kids kicked harder and harder. They were all laughing, because whatever Cadence was saying to them, she obviously was making it fun.

She was clearly a great teacher. The kids were engaged, watching her with eagerness. She swiped at the splashes hitting her square in the face and clapped her hands for the good job they'd done.

That's when he straightened from the bench and marched down the aisle, moving around the bleacher benches on his crutches to avoid moms and smaller kids sitting together in various stages of contentment. He didn't look over his shoulder as he hit the doorway to the stairs leading down to the main floor. He knew if he did look back, then everything he had said to Cadence in the shadow-filled parking lot would have blown up in smoke.

Put the past behind him. Sure, how was he going to do that when he couldn't stop noticing the woman she'd become? Because she'd followed her destiny, he reminded himself as he navigated the concrete stairs. She'd followed the path God had put before her, and that path was a world apart from the one he'd been called to follow.

The good Lord had known what Ben had needed, and the moment he'd signed up for the physical stamina test to qualify for the pararescue jumper program—similar to the brutal week of training for SEALs—he'd been hooked. It was a perfect fit, as if all his life he'd been training for this job in the military. He was a natural outdoorsman; he could track, hunt, shoot, evade, swim, run and dive.

After finishing the Pipeline—the series of schools in his year and a half of training—he'd been happy. He loved training. He loved his first real combat mission so much, he'd been certain he'd found his destiny.

And had left Cadence to find hers.

Questions troubled him, but what had happened to her life since they parted was not his business. He was here because he couldn't say no to his sisters. Because he knew Amy's budget was tight with making ends meet. She had to manage Westin's medical bills, largely from the hospital stay after he'd been swept away in the river, and plan a wedding.

He was glad to watch the kid and save her the cost of a babysitter. He'd been equally happy to pay for the lessons—not that he'd told her yet that he'd laid down his own cash.

Ten more minutes. He'd meet Westin in the boys' locker room, get him dressed and they'd hit a burger place. He'd seen a drive-in just down the street. He didn't get a lot of bacon cheeseburgers where he'd been deployed. But the thought of food didn't prove a good substitute for his earlier thoughts.

The main entryway was loud with the sounds of kids hauling rolled towels, coming and going with little supervision—or so it seemed. Moms with infants and toddlers struggled to dole out enough change for the pop machine or search through their bag for some necessary item for swim class.

The front desk was busy. A line had formed, but he didn't pay the folks there much attention as he passed. Until he heard a snippet of conversation that seemed to rise above the background din. "I had heard Cadence Chapman would consider taking another student, and we've driven all the way up from Wyoming."

Out of the corner of his eye he saw the woman and her daughter. She couldn't have been more than twelve or thirteen, with braces on her slight overbite and her dark hair pulled back into a ballerina kind of bun. She was coltish and lean, and reality punched him in the gut.

Cadence's years of competition diving were not behind her. She was a coach now. A teacher. She'd never left the sport, even here in this rural spot on the map. Why? She'd probably retired from the fast-track life and had opted for a simpler life.

But that still didn't explain why she was working **at** the county pool, at the county's pay scale, which he would guess was far from impressive.

Stop wondering about it. Wondering would lead only to thinking about her more. She might have grown up and come back to her roots, but she was still the same, he realized. Competitive, driven and looking for glory. Why else would a former world-class athlete coach others, if not to compete vicariously through them?

He didn't know. And he was half ashamed of his less-than-complimentary-thoughts about her. The past isn't buried as well as you think, man. He had his own issues, he knew. It was hard being second best to her dreams—so much so that it still hurt. Maybe that was why he'd never been able to have a long-term relationship with a woman.

He was a great dater. He'd been on a lot of first dates and second dates. Third dates and tenth dates. But he'd never gotten to a higher level than that. He always blamed it on his job. He'd been deployed nine months out of the year for most of his career.

But since the recent Iraq war he'd been home to Florida only once before being wounded in combat. Relationships took time and commitment, and he'd never had that to offer any woman.

Now he wondered how much his perpetual bachelor state had to do with being burned so hard and so bitterly when Cadence chose her diving. Of course, he'd pushed her away first, but a part of him knew that if it were real love, nothing could break it. Guess it wasn't real love. At least not on her part. Love brought with it too much hurt. Too much loss. And enough rejection to sour a man on love for a lifetime. He never wanted to be second fiddle again.

Since he had time to spare, he studied the pool schedule. Maybe he'd bring Westin in for public swim time so the kid could have fun in the water again without worrying about a river's powerful current. He noticed the mom and young teenage girl had been given a pamphlet of information, which they were busy reading.

Time was up, so he headed for the boys' showers. Through the open door onto the deck he could see a large slice of the pool. There was Cadence, her back to him as she helped her students climb the ladder. She waved goodbye to them. Eyes shining as they went to their respective shower rooms, the kids clearly had had fun.

Westin burst through the door. "Uncle Ben! I blew the biggest bubbles. Did ya see?"

"I saw some big bubbles, buddy. And a few really cool kicks, too." It was good seeing his nephew excited again.

"Did you know that the middle of galaxies are just like a drain?"

"I know. Go take a shower. Go on."

"You do? It's cuz of gravity." Westin hopped into the showers, which were all running thanks to the stream of boys coming in and out of the pool.

Westin dunked his head and called it good, water dripping down his face as he grabbed Ben's crutch. Ben had to be extra careful not to slip. A pool employee came in, took one look at him on crutches on the wet floor and went pale. The man didn't know that walking like this was a piece of cake, considering. He worked his crutches expertly on the slick floor without a single skid.

Westin led the way to his locker, while Ben got out the kid's dry clothes and wrapped up the towel and dripping swimsuit. Westin was talking a mile a minute about everything he'd done in class, how he'd already made a friend named Jacob and how nice his swim teacher was.

Cadence. Since there was no easy way he was ever going to get her out of his mind, he gave up the battle. She was Westin's teacher. That's all there was to it.

What troubled him the most was that if the past was buried, what was this ache lodged like a fist behind his sternum? He'd never been good at emotions, but he was afraid to take these out into the light and look at them. He figured it was best to leave them in the dark, where he could pretend he didn't feel them. If he didn't examine his feelings, then he could fool himself into thinking they weren't something like affection at all, but something curable…like acid reflux.

Right, he scoffed at himself, and followed Westin out the door. And as if heaven was offering him a great big you-can't-miss-this sign, light through the high window fell in a diagonal shaft of gold over a petite woman wearing a sweatshirt and a pair of shorts. With a small backpack hooked over one shoulder, a bottle of water in one hand, she turned to say goodbye to Peggy at the front desk, her sleek black ponytail bouncing as she turned her head. Her steps were graceful and sure.

Ben swore the light followed her as if to say, "She's the one."

Time was suspended as she strolled through the milling crowd and out the door, the bright sunshine swallowing her as she disappeared from his sight. But not from his mind.

She's not the one, he argued with himself firmly. Anything that made him think otherwise was simply a trick of light. A coincidence that had no bearing on his future. How could it be? The Lord had given him a path that made relationships practically impossible.

She's not the one. He continued to argue with himself as he followed Westin outside into the baking heat of the noontime sun.

"Uncle Ben! Can I play on the slide? Can I? Can I? Please?"

He hadn't noticed the playground equipment on the grassy knoll of the county land. There was everything from swing sets to monkey bars to slides of various heights. "What about a hamburger?"

"I'm not starved yet. I could slide down that big one a few times first," Westin pleaded with wide, hopeful eyes.

"Okay. Turn off the Bambi eyes and go play. Give me your stuff."

"Wow! Thanks." Westin handed over his backpack lickety-split and took off, running with little-boy energy.

Right in the direction where Cadence sat on one of the many benches beneath the shade of a maple tree, a book in hand.

Maybe if he stayed back here she wouldn't notice him. Maybe if he edged a little more into the shadow of the building, he'd remain unseen. And then there would be no more chances for heaven to send him signals he had to ignore.

Chapter Eight

Cadence felt his presence, as warm and soothing as the dappled mix of shade and sunlight on her shoulders. She spotted him moving in the shadows near the building. Ben had frozen, crutches poised for his next step, and their gazes locked.

He's not the one, Cadence. She had to remind herself, because the wish rising within her was simply out of place. She'd learned to be practical the hard way.

Now, when she dreamed, it was for what could reasonably be found. A hot cup of sweetened chamomile tea on a lonely night. A good book to read over the weekend. A job that mattered. Friends to care about. Those were the dreams she carefully cultivated these days.

She kept those dreams firmly in place as he pasted a resigned look on his handsome face and smoothly crossed the roll of lush green grass on his crutches. A kid's duffel swung from his shoulder as he went, competent despite the bag he carried.

Before she could wonder if his nephew was playing somewhere on the playground, a call rang out. "Look at me, Uncle Ben! I'm on the biggest one!"

"I see, buddy." Ben stopped to acknowledge the cute little boy atop the tallest slide. He stood at attention while Westin swooshed down the metal ramp. The old equipment groaned at the seams, but Westin seemed to enjoy his ride all the same.

"Awesome! I'm gonna do that again!" He was on his feet, running to the short line at the ladder.

Ben chuckled, and there was no mistaking the fact that he loved his nephew. When he turned to her, that rare emotion lighting him up faded into shadow. "I don't want to interrupt your lunch hour."

"It's okay." She slipped a bookmark between the pages and closed the cover. "You didn't come to lap swim this morning. I thought after your let-the-past-lie speech that I might see you."

"I'm swimming in the evenings." He turned away, as if to watch his nephew take his turn on the slide. But his jaw tensed, and a muscle twitched along his neck.

He didn't seem to see Westin, who did a "yeah!" with an air punch when he landed on his feet in the sand. "My let-the-past-lie speech?"

"Yep. The past is already over, Ben. I agree with you, by the way. We ought to at least be friendly. I always wished you well."

He swallowed hard. "That's what I always wanted for you. Your happiness. For things to go your way."

"Well, they didn't do that, but everything turned out for the best."

"You mean the sole bronze you took in the Atlanta Olympics?" He glanced at her sideways, as if he were half afraid of her reaction, for it had been a disgraceful performance, according to so very many people.

She hadn't been at her best at that time, it was true. She couldn't deny the fact. "You saw that, huh?"

"I tried to keep track of you. You look surprised that I would."

"I know diving isn't your thing. You're more of a hockey kind of guy."

"I wanted to see you compete. Just because I thought that we shouldn't be together didn't mean I didn't care." He cleared his throat, as if to hide the emotion in his voice.

Emotion she heard. She'd thought all this time that he hadn't cared. It helped somehow, when she looked back on those tough years before and after Atlanta, to know there was some affection that had been genuine.

She almost forgot to distrust him. "I hear you became quite a soldier, and you did great things. That's how you were hurt?"

"Shrapnel, bullet—nothing heroic, believe me. My team was rescuing a downed chopper pilot who'd fallen into enemy hands. We don't take too kindly to our men being captured." He shot her a cocky grin, dimpled and confident, but the darkness in his eyes said otherwise. It said that he'd been behind enemy lines and it had not been easy or without cost.

Respect filled her so that it was hard to breathe. Ben had found the best in himself. Trying to hide the rush of pride for him, she slipped her book into her bag and scooted over to make plenty of room on the bench. "Would you care to join me?"

"As long as you plan on sharing your lunch, too."

"I have a baggie of cookies I'll let you pilfer."

"Then we have a deal." He eased over to the bench and lowered his crutches to the ground. The boards creaked as he settled beside her. "What kind of cookies?"

"Chocolate chip. What else?" She bent to search through her lunch sack and produced the promised baggie. "Toll House. I made them last night."

"This is what an Olympic gold medalist does with her Sunday nights?"

"Surprisingly."

It seemed like a lifetime since he'd sunk his teeth into one of Cadence's homemade cookies, but it had been worth the wait.

Moist and soft, doughy and laden with melted milk-chocolate chunks. Not even Rachel's cookies were this good. "This doesn't seem fair."

"Why not?"

"I get these great cookies, but all you get is my sorry company." His comment did what it was meant to do—make her smile.

"We all have our crosses to bear." With a casual shrug she popped a pint container of milk from her lunch sack and broke it open. "It must be a change for you to be home. I hear military life is very regimented."

"True, but my squad and I manage to keep things pretty real when our deployments end. So what about you? Being back home in Montana has to be a change to what you've gotten used to. Gold medals and fame."

She tipped her head back to drink from the carton. And he had to wonder if she deliberately took her time, swallowing and dabbing the corners of her mouth with a paper napkin. She delayed answering for so long, Westin had the chance to make two revolutions from the top of the slide to the bottom. Ben figured she simply wouldn't answer at all.

Maybe she didn't want to admit her life hadn't been everything she'd hoped it would be. Broadcasting or something equally high profile and lucrative. Coaching and teaching, he figured, paid well at the top training facilities in the country. Maybe she'd gotten burned-out on a big-city lifestyle and world-class importance. Maybe she figured a guy like him wouldn't understand.

"Coming back here was a necessity, not necessarily a choice. More like an embarrassment," she added, surprising him, her voice dipping with unmistakable pain. She paused and leaned forward, setting the milk carton in the grass as if it took all her concentration.

That's when he noticed her hand was trembling, betraying her. She wasn't kidding, and this wasn't the answer he was expecting. Suddenly the older sedan she drove and the discount-store flip-flops on her feet had new meaning.

He'd been wrong. So very wrong.

"Why a necessity?" he asked, although

it was the other thing she'd said—she'd come back home in embarrassment—that he really wanted answered. But the look on her face—maybe not exactly of agony or defeat…regret?—drew him.

The dappled sunlight caressed the creamy fine curve of her face, as if in comfort. And his heart, not good at feeling much of anything, tore wide open as if he'd taken a direct hit to the chest from a sixty-caliber weapon.

Pain. Shame. Defeat. That's what was on her face as she turned away, pretending to watch kids on the swing set rocking in high swoops in the bright, clean air.

"I was bankrupt." There. She'd said it. The first confession of a long series of painful secrets, which probably weren't so secret to anyone who bothered to dig up her past. But here in Montana, she didn't speak of what had happened to her in the rugged urban landscapes of Boston and Chicago. "I didn't have two pennies to rub together. I had to ask my mom for money so I could come home to stay. That surprises you, doesn't it?"

"A little." He tried to hide his reaction,

for her benefit, but she could see it. He didn't want to admit how shocked he was, and he hid it well. Only the brief flare of his nostrils as he inhaled gave him away.

He alone had been privy to her very extensive plans for the future—financial security being third only to winning a gold medal and getting out of rural Montana forever.

"Things didn't work out like I planned."

It was hard to admit, but it was the details she didn't want to talk about. She'd locked away those painful details in a dark corner of her soul. Sometimes it was the best way to go on living. To never look at the defeats and mistakes and go on as if they hadn't happened. Or at least to go on the best that she was able. A good psychologist might not think this the wisest plan, but it had kept her together when despair had seemed to sap all the light from her world. Especially when she'd had to buy back her Olympic medals from the bank.

"But how did you…?" He raked his fingers through his hair. Then he spoke again. "No, it's not my business. I'm sorry that happened."

"Thanks. Me, too. But a lot of good came out of it. I'm happy here. Happier than I thought I would be. I love my life, so what is it that they say? All things happen for a reason."

"You got hurt."

She shook her head, moving to the far edge of the bench. "I was naive and I needed to learn a lesson."

"But you were hurt." He came to her, warm as the summer breeze, as soothing as the shade. He was a friend when he was the last man she wanted as a friend. His hand curled around her nape, touching her the way he always used to when she was hurting or upset, her head down. And his fingers now were thicker, stronger, surer as he kneaded at the tension coiled tight.

I don't want to care about you again. She squeezed her eyes shut and willed with all her heart not to feel. Not to let him affect her. But then he stopped kneading and smoothed the escaped strands of hair away from the side of her face and leaned closer.

Her heart seemed to cease. Her lungs stalled. Everything within her stilled. He leaned closer still until his kiss shivered along the curve of her cheek. His lips were warm rough velvet, his caring like a gentle touch in the darkness. The tenderness lanced through her as if she'd taken a blow.

Why, after all this time, could Ben stir the very essence of her soul?

She used to think they were made for one another. A match made by God Himself. Two lonely people, a little lost, both having buried parents, without much of a home life to speak of. So why now, when they were more like strangers, did she feel his spirit somehow against hers, like melody and harmony? She could not stop the beauty of it flowing through her. The brief, eternal moment of connection between two hearts.

"It's not my business," he said quietly, but as firmly as the earth beneath her feet. "But I gotta know. What happened? You went to college. You competed. You won medals. I saw you do it."

"I thought it was the winning that was important. It was, and it enabled me to be able to continue training."

"Endorsements?"

She nodded. "I didn't get the kind of money the gymnasts and the more commercial sports saw, but it was enough. I could train. I earned my degree in physical ed, just like I wanted, and also in journalism."

"Just like you planned."

"Sort of. I was living in Chicago, and I was on track for everything I wanted. But I guess I just got so wrapped up in everything. Or maybe it was that I never stopped being a Montana country girl at heart. I believed people were good."

"Not everyone is." His voice broke with certainty. "I have a job because there are men who do bad things in this world. And I'm paid to stop them."

"You have a noble profession."

"I carry an automatic weapon and I use it. It's not noble. It's necessary." His hand covered hers. "What happened?"

"I didn't win in '96." She opened her eyes. The world around her was so beautiful it hurt to look at it—the blazing sun, the velvety grass, the sky so blue it could all have been a dream.

But it was real, she was here and she was

grateful. Those days so long ago in a cold and gray city had been bleak. "I trained, but I really wanted to ease into broadcasting, you know. I listened to the wrong people. People who seemed fine on the outside. My trainers, my coaches, my sponsors, everyone."

"But they had their own agendas?"

He sounded so understanding, it brought tears to her eyes. "They were like family, a family I'd never had. I wasn't alone after Barcelona, where I dove so perfectly. I had plans, they had plans, and I let myself get distracted from the fact that I simply loved to dive."

"You always have."

"Yes. And I still love everything about it. The training, the solitude. The moment of grace and grit of leaping high off the platform and flying. Of being weightless and free and the struggle to be perfect. Not in a rigid way, but in the chance to do one thing exactly right. It's like pureness. A goodness. Like one moment of beauty. I don't know. And then the wet kiss of the water and the slice of it. And the joy of knowing you get to do it all over again. I had lost that somehow. And I failed in Atlanta. I just...*failed*."

"But you got a medal. I saw you do it." He sounded sheepish, as if a tough guy like him had a hard time confessing to watching women's diving.

"I got a bronze on the springboard. Of all my medals, it is my second favorite."

"Second?"

"The first being the first medal I ever won, which was a gold. It was a dream I could touch. But the bronze in Atlanta—I had to work so hard for it. I've never had to work so hard for anything. I was failing, I was coming apart. My new family was coming apart, and they had their own motives I was only then beginning to see."

Looking back, it seemed so simple. So easy. How she'd actually felt as if she'd found her niche, what she'd been made to do. Her days were spent doing everything she loved. Swimming and training and gym work and pool work. And, always, the diving.

Her spirit rose at the memories of hour after hour spent diving—stretching for the sky and then the water. Working so hard at what she loved, it didn't seem like work at all. Peace had filled her, a peace she would never have imagined existed, except she was living it.

Everything seemed right, as if the Lord had brought her to her greatest happiness. The people surrounding her had behaved so wonderfully toward her. She hadn't seen the end coming.

"And after I came in third, my life changed and I learned exactly what mattered in life. And it wasn't a big sports endorsement or a contract with a network or being treated like someone important. Those people abandoned me, and my manager stole my money. I had nothing. Nothing, and a whole lot of bills to pay. I'm still paying off a part of the bankruptcy."

She looked off into the distance, as if the view of the rugged mountains, so stunning and larger than life, could offer some solace. "My fiancé left me. I lost everything and came home in disgrace. Nobody really knows, not around here. I'm not hiding the truth—I just wanted to leave it behind."

"I know how much your dreams meant to you."

"I shouldn't have told you." She with-drew her hand, breaking the connection between them and making it clear she didn't want his sympathy. She didn't need any act of comfort. "It seems like a long time ago in a world far, far away."

He felt her sadness like his own. The loss of innocence. It must have been hard on her. "A lot of people who had lost ev-erything might be bitter and broken. So, tell me how come you're more lovely and enchanting than ever?"

"You don't need to try to be charming to make me feel better." Her eyes filled and she bolted forward, gathering up her duffel and lunch and milk carton in one graceful, rapid swoop. She was on her feet, swiping at the stray wisps of her hair as if they were the problem and not the tears threatening to fall. "I can't talk about this anymore. I've got to go—"

"Wait. I don't understand." He stood, leaving his crutches behind to hobble to-ward her. "If I've upset you—"

"No." She held up her hand to stop him. "I can't let you keep complimenting me like that, because then I'm simply going to appreciate you all the more, Ben McKaslin. You and I both agree we can't go back." She slung the bag's strap over one shoulder and tucked her lunch sack away. "Keep the cookies. I guess I'll see you around."

The last thing she wanted to do was open up her heart some more and let this man who'd done so well with his life see how she'd been so foolish. Well, she no longer pretended to be anything more than the Montana girl she was meant to be. It was how God had made her—it was the place He'd brought her back to. And it was here that she had a life that mattered.

It was a small life, sure, with no far-reaching scope, but it was hers and it was full of purpose.

She didn't know what Ben thought of her as she turned her back and walked away. She wanted to tell herself that his opinion didn't matter. That she didn't care. But then she'd be lying to herself, and that was something she never wanted to do again.

So she kept walking—forward, not back.

* * *

Throughout the day the same hard-edged, shaky feeling overtook her, as if she'd made a terrible mistake. It wasn't that she'd spoken of times she'd rather have kept to herself, because the burden of her mistake still troubled her. It was made five times worse that Ben knew.

Ben, who'd left her because he couldn't hold either of them back. Ben, whom she'd told out of hurt at his need for freedom that she had bigger and better dreams than marrying him. Ben knew how hard she'd worked and trained, how earnestly she believed a rural Montana girl who loved to dive could be like the athletes she saw on the old black-and-white TV.

He would never know how she'd still succeeded, and if she had little to show for it, then working earnestly for what she'd excelled at had somehow made her whole. She'd grabbed her dream, and it wasn't a gold medal. No one could take away what she'd earned. What she'd done. What she loved.

After the hours of public swim she

stayed late, enjoying the lull before water aerobics, swim team practice and then the evening schedule. With the doors locked and Peggy in the office doing paperwork, Cadence was officially off the clock as she climbed the ladder.

The higher she ascended, the calmer it became. The slosh and gurgle of the pool water became a pleasant background noise. High up in the rafters the sound echoed like a hushed blessing. She breathed in the peace. The calm.

The platform's textured surface was dry and rough against her bare feet. For her, it was the closest thing to touching heaven as she curled her toes over the edge and stretched her arms overhead. The energy pulled through from the soles of her feet to the tips of her fingers. For one long moment she visualized the dive in her head before she pulled her arms down and sprang with just enough power.

Her feet left the platform, and she flew through the air toward the rafters in one perfect moment before gravity caught her, pulling her down to the smooth water below. She tucked without thought, bringing her nose toward her belly button and her arms to her knees.

Weightless and free, she somersaulted two full revolutions, gaining speed, weightless as she saw the water fast approaching through the tiny space between her pointed feet. She stretched out again, pure joy, feeling her fingertips slice through the water, cool and refreshing as it welcomed her home, sluicing across her skin from forehead to toes. She heard the smallest splash and popped to the surface, smiling from the inside out.

Her life might be far from what she'd envisioned while training in this same pool when she was in junior high. The long hours. The grit and sacrifice and discipline. The injuries she'd come back from and the losses.

Oh, the losses. Her father's death. Her chance for happiness with Ben. The rejection by those she was closest to when she'd failed to bring fame and more money to them after the Atlanta Games. The man she'd loved with a pure and devoted heart—Tom—had walked away when he'd found out there were no millions. Not even pennies to rub together.

But she was content with her life so far, she thought as she climbed from the pool. Water dripping, she grabbed the metal rails and climbed into the rafters.

There were people with worse trials in their lives. Everyone had a bumpy path. It was part of life, for there was balance in all things. It was how God had made the universe in His infinite wisdom. Dark and light. Sadness and joy. Bitter and sweet.

She was proud to have been able to know the hardships, too, because it reminded her so well how gracious God truly was. She knew that for a fact as she turned around on the edge of the board, so she was standing on only the balls of her feet. Her arms were at her sides as she bounced and waited for just the right moment.

She left the platform, tumbling, falling. God had given her this blessing, this love of diving, to help get her through the down times, the hardships, those tough bumps in the road. To give her hope for the good things He had in store for her.

She was patient and she believed. As

she broke the surface, kicking toward the ladder, she vowed she would never forget to count her blessings.

Chapter Nine

He couldn't get Cadence and her confession out of his mind. He tried everything— pitching in at the diner, grilling and cleaning and even whittling down Paige's "minor repairs needed" list, which kept him busy but wasn't demanding enough to keep his mind focused.

Thoughts of Cadence kept creeping in. So the older car, less expensive clothes and sack lunch were explained. Now he knew why she was here teaching swimming at the public pool for a pittance, when she could probably make so much more coaching or teaching diving.

But she'd come home to Montana because it was all she had. What she knew.

To a lot of folks in these parts, it wasn't the material things that mattered, but heart and integrity. He respected her for her life and her choices. And her losses.

What kind of man would walk away from Cadence, whether she had money in the bank or not a penny to her name? Rage flashed red until it was all he could see. What kind of fiancé was he that he didn't protect her from people out to use her? Didn't hunt down her manager and demand every cent of her earnings back. What kind of man could stop loving Cadence?

Heaven knew he'd never been able to.

Which was why he needed to keep a wide berth between them. And why he needed to stop thinking of her every waking second of the day.

It didn't help that Amy had sweet-talked him into taking Westin to his daily lessons. If he bailed out, then it was up to Rachel, who had enough on her plate, since she lacked the capacity to say no to anyone. So there was no solution but to sit on the bleachers in the observation balcony and watch his nephew, because Westin had begged him to and he loved the little guy.

Watching Cadence for half an hour was tough going. It was impossible not to notice her. His gaze was drawn to her like the earth to the moon, and it was as if the old ties were still between them, the unexplainable emotional bond more powerful than gravity could ever be, when once she was the center of his world.

At least he had his answers. At least he knew what had become of her, what had changed her. In his job he'd seen more than enough heartache and desperation and evil, and it saddened him that even a hint of that had touched her life. Angered him that anyone had dared to hurt her when she was like a wish come true, still loving and gentle and good after all she'd been through.

Long ago he'd feared that success—because he knew she would go far with her diving—would change her, would rip them apart if he stayed with her. He'd been so sure that a small-town Montana boy would not be good enough for her, when in fact, he was the one who'd done the changing. Not her.

It was an odd thing to see her teach

swimming, the same as she'd done when she was a teenager needing money for her training. She still scrunched up her face and blew bubbles into the water with the kids. She clapped and congratulated and won the adoration of every one of her students. She still grabbed the wall, stretched out alongside them and kicked so they splashed as hard as they could.

The bitter man he'd become shamed him, but he endured the shame. Sitting on the top seat of the bleachers, hidden in the corner, he tried not to admit he wanted to love her. Who was he to love anyone? He had nothing to offer. He was terrible at relationships. There was no future between them. They'd already tested out that theory.

Frustration motivated him, and that was great for his training. He had started attending the scheduled evening lap swims and his leg was getting stronger. So he signed up to use the county gym, which was across the street from the pool building. He exerted himself until no thoughts of her could survive the fierce workout and his physical exhaustion.

Even then, when he slept, his mind would betray him and he'd see Cadence in his dreams, with the sunlight burnishing her dark hair, and as vibrant as a midsummer's day, laughing just for him. And it would affect him through the morning. He'd catch himself daydreaming of nothing…except the sound of her laughter.

"Hey, slacker." Rachel peered at him through the pass-through window. "Where's the rest of table four's order?"

"Waiting for my expert cooking," he quipped, trying to hide the fact that he'd lost track of what he was doing.

Rachel feigned scolding. "C'mon, for what we pay you, we want our money's worth."

"I'm doing this for nothing."

"Well, then we're getting what we're paying for." She winked, her smile sweet as she turned at the sound of the bell above the front door. New customers to seat. "I'll be back."

"I'll have the whole order up."

"Promises, promises."

He didn't mind pitching in where he could. Amy's fiancé was the temporary morning cook, but Ben had offered to work so Amy and Heath could spend a morning together. It had been Rachel's suggestion, of course, since she was the ever-thoughtful one. He could see her welcoming customers he didn't recognize— out-of-staters, by the looks of them, on a family vacation to Yellowstone. Or maybe up north at Glacier.

Glacier. Now, there was a place he hadn't been to in way too long. It was a shame his leg wasn't up to hiking, because he'd love nothing more when he took off his apron than to hoof it up into the wilderness. It was like a second home to him. Memories tugged at the closed rooms in his heart. Images of the countless overnight treks spent first with his dad, then on his own in the national parks. Which had helped him excel in his PJ training.

Survival school had been a snap—he'd been surviving in the wilderness since he was a boy. He missed it now—the crisp mountain forests, the fresh musical streams, the chalk of dirt beneath his boots and the breathtaking solitude. Maybe when his leg was stronger, before he flew back to Florida, he'd take a long hike.

He filled the plates and had them waiting by the time Rachel returned. She clipped in a new order and thanked him as she loaded up. A movement through the window caught his attention.

Mr. Brisbane was ambling down the aisle, the first to arrive and the first to leave of the early-morning old-timers, and despite the time that had passed since the Second World War, he still walked with a military presence.

"Is there something I can do you for, Mr. Brisbane?"

"Next time you've got a free morning, drop by our table. The boys and I would like you to join us." He snapped a salute and continued on his way.

Ben blinked. Bacon sizzled and sausages snapped and egg whites began to bubble, but he couldn't seem to move. Brisbane and his buddies hadn't invited anyone new into their group since…well, for as long as he could remember.

"Hey, Ace, you'd better let me take over." Rachel was elbowing him out of the way and prying the spatula from his grip. "You look lost in thought. You wouldn't happen to be sad about not seeing a certain someone later this morning?"

Oh, he knew what she was up to. The best way to deal with her serious romantic view of the world was to head her off at the pass, before she could gain momentum on the downhill side. "I don't mind seeing Cadence a bit. It's good that we can be friendly after all these years."

"Friendly, huh?"

"What else can there be, when I'm leaving in, what, a month? Less if I can get my leg up to par." Speaking of which, his leg was killing him. He'd left his crutches up against the wall, thinking that it would be good for his leg to take weight for a few hours. A good idea, but his calf bones were complaining.

"You never know. Love is a tricky thing. She might want to actually put up with you this time." Rachel elbowed him over. "Go on. Maybe you should pack up a nice muffin basket and take it over to the pool?"

"Why? Amy and Heath are going to be there. I don't want to barge into their time."

"You should do it anyway. Friends do things like that all the time."

"Sure they do." He gave her ponytail a tug. "Trouble is, I got enough friends."

"Well, maybe you do. But what about Cadence?"

She has enough, too, he thought as he grabbed his crutches and got weight off his leg. He remembered how she'd had her softball team friends. She didn't need him. She didn't even want him. The fact that she'd practically run off from the bench outside the pool ought to be a clue.

He told himself that Rachel was simply being Rachel. She had a rosy view of the world, and he wasn't going to take her observation for real, because she'd seen Cadence at the pizza place, where she'd been surrounded by friends. She wasn't lonely. If anything, she was clearly uncomfortable around him—maybe as uncomfortable as he was around her.

It wasn't until he was coming out of the gym the next afternoon and negotiating the front steps with only one crutch that he realized what he had to do.

Sunlight glittered on the high windows

of the pool building across the wide expanse of grassy lawn, drawing his gaze. And, miraculously, through the fingers of sunlight shining into his eyes, he saw Cadence somersaulting in thin air.

For one shining moment she remained suspended in his sight, and then fell away as if riding a sunny beam.

He had his answer. He needed whatever those loose ends were between them tied up. He wanted the real story this time. The real reason she dived with perfection in a county pool and lived simply, instead of off somewhere using her expertise and her talent.

Since he was a man of action, he ditched his bag in his truck and prayed the pool's front doors were unlocked during off-hours. Of course they weren't, but he had a plan B. He was a PJ—he always had a plan.

Cadence looked over the top of her book to the clock on the corner of the crowded mantel. No wonder her stomach was growling. It was about time to forage for supper. The quiet piano music humming from the inexpensive CD player added serenity as she marked her page. She set the book on the rickety coffee table and climbed to her bare feet.

The town house was awfully quiet. She searched through the handful of movies she'd rented at a bargain price and popped an old favorite into the VCR. While Ingrid Bergman filled the screen, Cadence circled around the breakfast bar to the kitchen trying to figure out what she felt like eating. Tonight she had softball practice, and after that straight to bed, because she opened the pool lap swim, which meant her alarm went off at 4:45 a.m.

The doorbell jingled—that was a surprise. She wasn't expecting anyone, unless it was Mrs. Cranston who lived next door having trouble with her car again. Padding across the living room to the door in her bare feet and wearing her most comfortable relaxing clothes, she wasn't prepared for the face on the other side of the peephole.

Ben McKaslin.

How did he even know where she lived? Then she remembered he knew where her mother was, that it was easy to find her sister and brother—all he would have to do was look in the phone book. She'd twisted back the dead bolt before she'd even made the decision to invite him in. Not that she was dressed for it. She couldn't look anywhere near her best in a nearly worn-out T-shirt a size too big and knit shorts with a blueberry stain at the hem.

But it was too late to worry about that or to wonder at the sparkle of joy she felt as she pulled the door open and saw him, kissed by the bright glare of the sun. The hot wind ruffled his short dark hair. His steely gaze latched on to hers and she forgot about her appearance. Every thought fled straight from her head as the joy within her expanded.

He looked so good—not that she could see beyond the intense lock of his gaze. These are just old feelings, she tried to tell herself, and love long buried that still remained for this one man.

But then in the next instant she knew that wasn't right. Her entire being twinkled like star shine and this emotion she felt was entirely new. Entirely different. More strident than anything she'd felt before. It was as if he could see through every layer of her to her very soul.

"I hope you don't mind that I looked you up." His rugged baritone didn't sound the least bit apologetic or conciliatory. "I would have called, but I didn't want you to say no."

"I wouldn't have." She took a ragged breath, suddenly painfully aware of how she'd turned away from him that day on the bench. It felt long ago, but it was only a little more than a week. "Westin is making such good progress. He's my best bubble blower."

"He takes after his uncle." Dimples dug in, bracketing his tight smile. He was a fierce man—no, a strong man. Even when he smiled there was an intense male energy to Ben McKaslin that probably had women wishing for him on first stars of the night.

Not that she was going to let herself be one of them.

"I hope you haven't eaten yet." He gestured with his hands, and she realized he held two restaurant food sacks. "I brought supper from the diner, thanks to Rachel and Paige. Are you gonna let me in?"

"I'm thinking of barring the door against you," she quipped, "but I'm betting that they trained you how to get through a locked door in the military."

"Not only am I trained to pick your lock, I can break it, shoot it, grenade it, explode it and call in an air strike."

"Wow. You're handy." Knowing she'd regret it if she let him in—and regret it more if she didn't—she held the door open wide. "Come in. You never told me what you did in the military."

"I did a lot of things. Rescued downed pilots and hostages and rendered medical aid or military might, depending. I was often dispatched with SEAL teams or on Delta missions—counterterrorism stuff. Most of it is classified." He ambled in without any crutches, but he had a serious limp. "This is a nice place you have."

"It's home."

A modest answer—he should have expected it. In fact, he'd expected a small place, considering her bankruptcy and all. But it was nice—sunny and feminine, something Rachel would have liked. With frilly curtains at the windows and flowery pillows on the couch. Vases of fake flowers and porcelain figurines in a lighted glass case next to the decades-old TV. He thought of his big screen and satellite dish he was never home on the base to watch.

He'd thought about a lot of things he had and she didn't, and many things he should have done and hadn't.

"No gold medals on display?"

"They're in my safe deposit box. The kitchen's this way." She snatched one of the sacks from him. It was heavy—milkshakes? she wondered, and unrolled the top. The sight of the paper cups and plastic lids—and the chocolate shakes beneath—answered her question. "You still want to be friendly?"

"Why not?" He set his sack on the edge of the round farmhouse-style table, his gaze meeting hers.

He felt an undeniable catch in his chest. He couldn't chalk it up to indigestion, arrhythmia or some physical malady, and he wasn't about to consider anything as ridiculous as love. That was impossible.

He knew only that he needed these ends tied up. "You were right. I agree with what you said about us. We can't go back. But we can go forward."

"Forward?"

He reached into the sack and handed her the bacon cheeseburger—just the way she used to like it—then took out one for himself. "Friends. I wish I'd had the guts to tell you last time we talked. I like who you were and I like who you are now. In case you haven't noticed, I don't have a lot of friends around here. Unless you count my sisters, and they have to like me."

"Friends, huh?" She kept her head turned away from him as she padded around the counter into the small U-shaped kitchen, where cute canisters lined up from small to large sat on the beige counter.

Tidy place. A cookie jar in the shape of a cartoon whale centered the small space between the stove and the sink. Frilly hand towels and hot pads hung from various spots. She was settled here; she was at home here. And he didn't know why he felt as if he'd been punched in the chest.

It wasn't regrets over the past that bugged him. It was what could happen between them in the future.

And how impossible was that?

Cadence grabbed a plain white roll of paper towels and carried it with her on her way back from the corner cupboard. She set two flower-edged plates on the table and slid one across the lace cloth in his direction.

He hadn't had a home since his mom and dad died, and that was too long. Pain radiated through his lungs and he managed to drag in a wheezy breath, reminiscent of his boyhood days of asthma. But like his grief, he'd grown out of it.

"I've been living out of a rucksack since I left for boot camp," he found himself saying as he set the tub of fries in the middle of the table and hauled out two large containers of tartar sauce and ketchup. He nudged the ketchup in her direction.

"I'm usually deployed nine months of the year—until we went to Afghanistan, and then it's been 24/7 for the last few years. And now—" he glanced down at his scarred leg with frustration "—pins and plates and two surgeries later, here I am in Montana."

"But you're off your crutches."

"Yep. I bet you know something about that."

"Crutches?" Her stomach dropped, and to hide her surprise she ripped the paper off her straw and inserted it into the top of the plastic cup lid. "How did you know?"

"I watch the sports channels. I read sports sections. I know you dived injured in Atlanta."

"And why I was lucky to get the bronze." She didn't know why it mattered, why she attributed it to thoughtfulness on his part when he'd probably only stumbled across news of her career in the newspaper. It moved her nonetheless.

Her throat ached and she didn't trust her voice, so she took a pull on the straw. Rich, creamy chocolate shake made the old-fashioned way caressed her tongue, but it didn't smooth away the emotion. "I was six months out of a hip replacement."

She closed her eyes against the remembered images of the training accident— she'd been practicing her initial new dives on a trampoline, which was commonplace enough in her training routine. She'd been wearing her safety harness and the safety nets were up and in place, but she'd gotten hurt anyway, which she did a lot in her sport. "It was almost as painful as when I cracked my skull when I didn't leap out far enough and did a backward flip onto the platform."

"And I thought getting hit with shrapnel from a grenade was harrowing." He folded his hands. "Do you want to say grace?"

"You're the guest, so go ahead."

When he spoke, it was as if the timbre of his voice moved through her like a morning breeze. As if a light went on inside her soul like the gentle touch of dawn. His simple blessing was brief and she could barely manage to clear away the tangle of raw emotions in her throat in time to say amen.

Did he feel this, too? she wondered, her heart filling, even as she bid it not to. Even as she tried to hold back the tide of affection she did not want to feel. New emotions for Ben—respect, admiration, awe—left her too confused to speak as he told her about Amy's fiancé, who'd lost his wife and son in a house fire. Heath had walked away from his life and from living—until he'd happened into their family's diner and fell in love with Amy.

To fill the silence between them, Ben told how Rachel was still waiting for Mr. Right. How Paige's son was busy looking at colleges and studying for the SAT, hoping to score high enough to land a full scholarship.

He talked and she listened, struggling against the rising tides of her heart. He made her laugh, made her wish that there could have been a happily ever after for the two of them. Together and not apart.

She knew how wonderful Ben's tenderness had been so long ago. He'd always been gentle with her and treated her like a lady, always with respect.

How much more wonderful would the mature Ben be?

Was it hopeless to wish that she could find out? It had been long hard years she'd spent alone, while either most of her friends had married or her married friends had had babies. She was over thirty. She wanted a husband and a family. But not just any husband.

She knew without having to ask that Ben was not, even now, husband material.

"Is that all you're gonna eat?" he asked in the low, intimate rumble of his, the one that stirred her soul and nourished her dreams. She nodded and he said, "Yeah? Then come walk with me."

He held out his big capable hand, palm up, his gaze tender and his heart in his eyes. How was she going to say no to that? Helpless and knowing better, she laid her fingers on his wide callused palm and said the only, inevitable answer. "Yes."

Chapter Ten

"Tell me about this fiancé. The one who left you when you ran into hard times."

Cadence shot Ben a sideways glance. With the sun in her eyes it was hard to make out exactly what emotion was on his face. Curiosity? Or was there more to his sudden question, she wondered as they walked side by side through the expansive parklike common area of her town house complex.

They weren't the only ones out enjoying the bright late-summer evening. Couples strolled hand in hand along the concrete path that circled the grounds, heading toward the grove of trees and a wetland pond.

"Do I have to tell you about Tom?"

"Nope. But then I won't tell you about Kit."

"Ooh, now you have me wondering. Who's Kit?"

"Spill your guts, and then I'll tell you." His voice dipped with sincerity.

How did he do it? she wondered. How could he radiate caring even as he teased? Her spirit rose even as she tried to keep her senses. Do not fall in love with him again, she commanded, although she feared it was already too late. She fought to keep her hopes down, because there were so many reasons she had to be sensible.

And only one reason that she should not.

Ben reached for her hand and tucked it into his much bigger one, holding her securely—not tight, but just right. Companionably. A perfect fit.

Don't even start wishing, Cadence.

She took a shivery breath, trying to ground herself when she saw several couples ahead of them stopping to feed the ducks that had taken up residence in the marshy waters. There was no mistaking the comfortable togetherness of the couples, their wedding rings glinting in the light.

What would it be like to be married, to have someone always at her back? To always have someone rooting for her, caring. Someone who would love her unconditionally. She'd never known. Before, with Ben, they'd both been too young to hold a mature love in their hearts. And with Tom—

"I was fooled by Tom." Embarrassment bit her like a Doberman and hung on. She couldn't shake it loose. She probably never would.

"Do I have to hunt this Tom down and punch him for you?"

"No, but it's the thought that counts."

"Not that I'd punch a civilian. But that's how I feel about anyone who would hurt you like that. I left you for two reasons. So you could follow your gold, and because I wasn't good for you." He cleared his throat, as if there was something he wasn't ready to say. "This Tom fellow. How long were you engaged?"

"We were planning the wedding after a year. That's an appropriate time to wait, you know." She stopped so she could watch the duck family paddle close to beg for more food. Couples complied by opening the plastic bags of bread crumbs or crackers they'd brought.

"The wedding was going to be after the Atlanta Games, and, well, there was no money, no guests and no groom. He told me that he hadn't signed on for this, meaning the bankruptcy, and I had reinjured my hip competing, so I had decided to retire. And here I had thought it was true love."

"He was a weak man. He didn't have what it takes to stick."

"He was a greedy man. I had some serious money in the bank. He just wanted to be a millionaire. That's what he said. After that I had to revise my theory of true love."

"You have a theory of true love?"

"Yes. True love is only real when it goes both ways. I had loved him deeply. But he didn't love me enough. See?"

He nodded and fell silent, as if thinking over her words.

The bird family had clustered together, the daddy duck looking dapper in his shimmering green accent feathers, working with the plainer brown mama duck to watch over their brood. They had ten ducklings, each looking as if they could fit in Cadence's palm. Their fluffy yellow-brown feathers made them look adorable as they snapped up bits of floating bread with their shiny bills.

"I am sorry that you were hurt, Cadence." His fingers squeezed hers just right, in a way that made her wishes rise higher. Like a helium balloon held back against a wind, it tugged at her.

"Tell me about Kit."

"Kit. Let's see." He gazed off at the horizon, where thunderheads gathered along the peaks of the nearby Bridger Mountains. "Not many men with my job marry. It's hard to keep a relationship going, and she was my biggest lesson why I shouldn't even try."

"Did you almost marry her?"

"Nope. I was about twenty-four. I'd been in the air force for about five years. Felt like maybe I was old enough to settle down. A lot of my buddies had gotten married. Not a lot of men in my squad, but it was tempting. To have someone to come home to. To have someone to share meals with. Someone to…turn to, I guess."

"You mean love."

"Yeah."

He stopped, waiting as another man and woman strolled hand in hand toward the pond. Their young grade-school children ran out from behind them. A little girl with golden curls bouncing every which way looked cute in a matching pink shirt-and-shorts set. Little pink sandals adorned her feet.

Her brother was older, black haired and blue-eyed, a charmer with dimples who outran his sister and shouted, "Mom! Mom! I get to feed 'em first!"

Then Ben spoke. "Sometimes a man thinks about kids. That it could be nice. But then there's the reality of the job. On date number eight, Kit started complaining that she missed me, that I was gone too much. On date, what, number twelve or so, she started saying how much she wanted to love me but how could she when I was gone so much."

"That's a lot to ask, considering your relationship was young."

"Yeah, but around date twenty I called it quits. She wanted me to look for another job in the military."

"That was one woman." She knew he was gun-shy. She knew that he'd been adrift since he'd lost his parents as a child.

"Not when I watched buddy after buddy of mine bail out of the PJs. I had to make a choice. Keep doing the job I think matters, the job God made me to do. Or give it up for a woman who isn't my true love."

"And a man like you believes in true love?"

"I do." He tugged her gently away from the pond, leading her through the lush grass. "I've learned that there's only one of those in a lifetime, and I'd already missed the chance at mine."

Had she heard him right? Cadence didn't dare breathe as her mind went over his words. Did he feel this, too, this vibrant shimmering emotion that was too new for love and too strong for friendship?

It was as if a long-dormant place within her soul, dark for so long, had begun to shine. How could she not fall irrevocably in love with him now?

"I start thinking about what I missed by making the choices I did," he went on, thoughtful. "I was just a kid. I'd turned eighteen and thought I knew everything. Thought I was indestructible. I was angry that life wasn't fair."

"I remember."

"But the decisions we make, even at that age—no, *especially* at that age—have far-reaching consequences."

"You chose defending this country instead of a quiet Montana life with me."

"I chose a solitary life, and I won't lie. There are times when I regret the aloneness."

Her eyes widened, growing bigger in her lovely face. Her hair was down and playing across her face. Her lovely, dear face that had filled his dreams and memories for most of his life.

What are you doing, man? he asked. His free hand, as if of its own free will, cupped the soft curve of her jaw and cheek, leaving his thumb free to caress the hint of a dimple in her dainty chin.

It started like a hard pain in his chest directly behind his sternum and exploded like a well-hidden land mine, flaring outward with a force of heat and energy that tore him apart. Love so shocking and powerful he could not stop the flow of it through the pieces of him. Sweet like honey, as devastating as molten lava, it filled his body and his soul, mending him and making him whole.

Don't let yourself love her, he commanded with all the strength of his will, but for the first time in his life, it wasn't enough. He couldn't stop this. Nothing could stop the emotion that was love, but the power of what he felt made the word pale in comparison. It was a fierce need to protect and provide for, a soul-engrossing devotion, tenderness so true and overwhelming that it made every fiber of his being hurt. Not from its pain, but from its brightness.

You're walking on dangerous ground, McKaslin. Drop her hand and walk away before both of you get hurt.

It was the only way he knew how to protect her. He took one long last glance at the people clustered around the marshy pond, feeding ducks. The sharp rising lilt of kids talking excitedly, the nasal, flat-noted quack of the ducks, the ripple of wind across water filled his senses. He couldn't ignore the happy-looking married couples holding hands or standing shoulder to shoulder, so close that their shadows joined as one.

An odd tingling skidded down his neck, and he looked down at his feet. At the shadows he and Cadence made on the lawn before them—shadows joined as one.

He took a step away, separating their images, but the emotion within did not cool or fade. It seemed to gain strength as he kept her hand snug in his and led her back to her building.

Back to their separate lives.

"Uncle Ben?"

"Yeah, buddy?" Ben ignored the scalding pain in his lower leg as he secured the final end pole and tugged the rope. His old pup tent rose like a shadow in the long white fingers of moonlight from the half-moon.

"Wow," Westin breathed, raspy with excitement. "That's cool! How long are you gonna stay?"

"Until my leg gets better." Ben pushed aside the sting of emotion as he whipped a knot in the rope, secure and low against the small metal stake he'd driven into the ground earlier. "I've got to be able to run really good on it."

"You can walk on it now." The kid sounded worried. Sad, because their time together was limited.

Yeah, buddy, I know how you feel. He held out his hands. "All done. You get the sleeping bags."

"Yeah! The one you bought me!" Westin, who'd chosen the stars-and-galaxy-themed sleeping bag, was distracted away from his earlier question as he raced to the patio where they'd stacked their overnight camping supplies.

There was nothing like braving the wilderness in your own backyard.

Rachel stood in the slider door, drawing it open, the overhead light falling softly around her. "I've got a treat fresh from the oven and marshmallow cocoa to go with it."

She laughed as Westin dropped the sleeping bags on the cement, torn between setting up the tent and eating sweets. "Finish setting up first, then come get the goodies, like real campers."

"'Kay!" Westin seized his bag and Ben's old one, and struggled with his burden across the back lawn.

A strange sense of déjà vu clicked over him as Ben watched them. Time was a funny thing, how it marched on and on without stopping, and yet there was a pattern to it. A cycle of life that somehow remained, if not the same, then similar.

He remembered this from his boyhood: Mom at the slider offering treats and Dad finishing up the tent. As a grade schooler, Ben had helped his dad set up, carry out the gear and roll out the sleeping bags. It was a dear thing, remembering how Dad had talked about tenting it with his dad. Granddad was gone. Dad was gone. And yet the cycle continued.

Cadence, the families he'd seen today, the uncertainty and trauma following his combat injuries—it was all adding up, making him take a look around, as if he could second-guess his choices.

Westin was struggling with a knot in the sack encasing his bag.

"Hand it here." He waited for the boy to nudge the bundle over and he took it, worked at the knot and handed it back. "Let's get these bags unrolled. I don't know about you, but I'd like some of Rachel's cookies."

They worked side by side, squeezed in the open flap of the pup tent, each on their side, rolling out their bags. For Ben, all it took was a flick of his wrist and his bag unrolled on its own.

But Westin was new to this, and the best way to learn was to do. He waited patiently while his nephew crawled on all fours to unroll his bag. He'd thought that having a son would sure be nice—it would be something like this.

Then again, how could it be when he'd been deployed nearly constantly for the past two years? Any wife and son he would have he'd see just as much as he saw his family here—a few holidays. Maybe a week here or there.

And then he'd be off with his M-203 and his squad, sleeping in places that made this little setup with the pup tent look like luxury.

"Uncle Ben? Do ya think my new dad'll know how to put up a tent?"

"You ask him and see, buddy. Your new dad seems all right."

"He's real nice and he makes Mom smile all the time. And he knows how to play baseball."

"Important stuff." Ben tried to swallow past the knot in his throat, but couldn't.

He tried not to think of more time passing. Of Westin and his new dad playing ball and camping in the backyard. Of them doing all the things a father and son ought to do.

Who knew the next time he'd be home again? Westin would be older, probably in Pee Wee football and church activities and he'd be calling Heath not "my new dad," but "my dad."

As it should be. But the time it was passing, and in Ben's life it was just another day. And another day. With no love to give it value.

Westin ran to the house full speed, to where Rachel waited, watching over him, ever the loving aunt. She leaned forward to chat with him, her eyes shining, looking so much like their mom it seemed to make everything worse.

Whatever he was longing for, he could not name it. He could not have it. He could only watch, heart laid open, as Westin accepted the brown paper grocery bag as if it were made of pure gold.

"Thanks, Aunt Rachel!" Westin's excitement echoed across the layers of the night.

"You're welcome, cutie." Rachel stood watching as the boy raced away from her, searching through the shadows until she caught sight of her big brother and waved.

He waved back. He watched as she tipped her head up to study the night sky, what little of it she could see from the glare of the inside lights.

"Uncle Ben! Look what we got! Aunt Rachel made s'mores for our cookies!"

"S'mores? All right."

Then Rachel called out, pointing upward. "Look! A falling star."

Ben spotted the flare of light winging across the velvet sky in an arc from heaven to earth. Memories welled, more images he did not want, more emotions he did not want to feel.

"That's not a falling star, Aunt Rachel,"

Westin, the resident astronomy expert, piped up with all the authority of his seven years. "It's just junk. Stuff like dust 'n ice and space chunks smashing into us, and our atmosphere burns it up."

"It's not romantic to wish on burning-up space chunks, Professor Westin." Rachel watched, waiting, until the streak of fire disappeared. "Besides, what else is there to wish on? When I was a little girl I used to wish on the first star of the evening, until your uncle Ben told me it wasn't a star at all but a planet and ruined that for me." She winked. "You two let me know if you need anything."

After wishing Rachel good-night, Ben tried to turn off his brain. Fiercely tried not to think of holding Cadence's hand and seeing their shadows joined. But it was hopeless. All through eating the s'mores and drinking the frothy cocoa and listening to Westin talk, at the back of his mind those thoughts remained.

And what good were those thoughts? They could only make him discontent. Soon he'd be back where the star-filled skies were lit up with tracer fire, and the rapid pop of automatic weapons peppered the night. He had his future decided. He had his duty to fulfill. He'd signed away his life to Uncle Sam.

Chapter Eleven

Friday was a crazy day, with it being the end of the swimming session. The kids were full of energy because the day was devoted to games appropriate for each class. Cadence watched Westin leap into the water and race with a kickboard the width of the pool, gaining ground for his relay team.

His classmates were shrieking, and she was calling encouragement to the swimmers as they struggled through the water. Weston was still very nervous of water. She could tell by his tension, but he was too much like his uncle to outwardly show it. He climbed out of the pool, handing over the board to Jacob, the last in line, who plopped into the pool and kicked with all his might.

The entire pool complex radiated noise—the three other graded beginner classes were having races, too, and the spectators in the stands added applause, stomping and cheers to the din.

The last day of classes was always Cadence's favorite. Her students had improved. She taught them important water safety all through the session, and seeing her kids having fun swimming made her proud. Everyone needed a purpose in life, and this was hers.

"Okay! Jacob and Kaylie, please stack the boards for me…and walk, don't run! Thank you." She grabbed her towel and hung it over her shoulders. "Here are your report cards. All of you were so awesome."

To each student she handed out the cards written in permanent ink and their guppy badges. She watched them walk off to the locker rooms, where their family members or caretakers waited.

She'd meant to find Ben in the stands, but she hadn't seen him. The other members of the McKaslin family—Westin's

mom and his new dad, Paige and Rachel—
had shown up to help celebrate the last day.
But as she scanned the stands, she saw they
were gone.

Westin's lessons had come to an end.
She knew that he hadn't signed up for the
next session, which started on Monday.
Remembering their kindness in the baseball park made her heart ache. There were
plenty of good people in the world—she
knew exactly how valuable they were.

When Ben's medical leave was done,
then she'd make an effort not to lose touch
with the McKaslin girls. There was always
the chance of catching Westin's T-ball
game if it didn't coincide with hers tomorrow. And there was no reason she couldn't
take them up on their offer to stop by the
diner just to say hi.

"Are you outta here?" Peggy asked, out
of breath, on her way to her advanced class
waiting quietly on the bench near the deep
end. "Be sure and stop by the front desk."

"Why? Hey, I turned in my paperwork."

"I didn't say you didn't." Peggy's eyes
twinkled as if she had a secret. "Just do it.
I'm your boss. Do what I say." She winked

and padded on, her attention already turning to her students.

What was that all about? Cadence wondered as she grabbed her clipboard and headed to the office. It was chaos—the last day always was. Moms and caretakers were there signing up at the last minute for Monday's session and the phone was ringing off the hook.

When she reached to pick up a line, the office manager, Sharon, gently nudged her away and pointed past the counter that looked out into the main area. There were friendly faces smiling at her—and waving. The McKaslins!

Her heart warmed as she waved back. She would get to say hello to them after all. She sneaked through the back door to avoid the crowd.

And that's when she saw Ben standing to the side holding a beautiful stained-glass vase brimming with cheerful yellow roses. There had to be two dozen of them, each bud tight and perfect, like drops of sunshine.

"For you," Ben said, and although they were in a crowded public place and his sisters were approaching and talking, all Cadence could see was Ben. The intimate look in his eyes that said he was glad to see her again.

Memories of their talk together and of their walk rolled through her head. The comfortable feel of her hand in his. The knowledge that it was enough just to be together. The unspoken hope she couldn't hold back. A wish that made no sense, for nothing had really changed. And yet the wish remained, for the heart had no logic, but a wisdom of its own.

The man Ben had become awed her, and it was as if the new room that he'd opened within her soul filled with the brightest light.

"We're so grateful to you," Amy was saying. "I never thought I'd see Westin back in the water again, and he so loves to play in the river. I wouldn't have tried swimming lessons so soon if it hadn't been for you."

Cadence blinked, forcing her gaze from Ben's, trying to make her brain think of normal things. It was way harder than it should have been. "Westin is the one doing all the work. He's made great progress. I graduated him to the second beginner class."

"We saw." Amy beamed with motherly pride. "And you *did* make the difference. Westin knew you were a friend of ours, that he could trust you. We didn't know of any other way to thank you. It was Ben's idea."

"Ben's, huh?" She saw the truth in his eyes. He was a thoughtful man—that didn't surprise her—but it was nice to be on the receiving end. Very nice. "Westin is a great kid. It was my pleasure to have him in my class."

"What are you doing this afternoon?" Rachel said, stepping forward, her eyes sparkling. "Say around four."

"I've got some private lessons until then."

"And it's what, a twenty-minute drive to our place from here?" Paige seemed to pick up on Rachel's lead. "That would work just fine. We won't be barbecuing until five."

"Westin's party." Ben leaned forward, dipping closer to explain. "Amy promised him a party if he stuck it out. He decided on burgers and ice cream cake. We're going to surprise him with presents. Make it a real celebration."

"You're his teacher—he expects you to come," Paige added.

"He'd be hurt if you didn't," Amy argued.

"Besides, you're a friend of the family." Rachel caught her by the hand and squeezed, a silent offer to renew their old friendship.

Could it be that her lonely days were over? That wish rose up within her, gaining height. Ben caught her hand in his, his touch like a question, one he could not ask.

And her heart answered instantly, irrationally, *yes*.

Ben knew the moment she arrived. There was a change in the air, like a shift of wind. Except that it came from inside him. As if the currents of his soul were pulled by her nearness, the way the moon tugged at the ocean tides. He was waiting to fill his eyes with the sight of her. And he wasn't disappointed. There she was appearing through the slider door and onto the sunlit patio.

She came!

Excitement punched hard in his chest, too hard to ignore or deny. He hadn't realized how much he'd wanted to see her.

She was dressed in a green blouse that made her blue eyes bright, crisp khaki shorts and sandals. Small, stylish sunglasses were pulled up on her head, holding her hair back from her face. Her hair was down from its usual ponytail, falling free around her shoulders, glinting blueblack in the direct sunlight.

She held a package in one hand, wrapped in festive paper and topped with a matching bow. While everyone called her name in greeting from the riverbank at the far edge of the lawn, she looked at him.

When her gaze latched on to his, brightness filled him and he could not look away. He was hardly aware of climbing up the bank and into the softer, hot grass of the yard. His feet could do nothing else but take him to her. His senses could do nothing else but become filled up with her. She was infinitely lovely to him. And her voice, when she spoke, was the most welcome of sounds.

"It is so good to see everybody," she said.

"Come on and join us!" Paige called from the floating cushion she'd tethered to the small wooden boat dock. "Pull up a cushion and come cool off. It's too hot over there."

"Yeah," Amy called from the shady dock, where she was stretched out reading alongside Heath. "There are extra towels on the picnic table."

Ben realized that he was halfway across the acre-sized back lawn. He'd left the pleasant shade, and the intense sun sizzled on his damp skin. He stepped on a small rock that ground into the bottom of his foot, but even pain slid into the background compared to how he felt when Cadence smiled at him.

"Rachel let me in," she explained to him as she snatched a big worn beach towel from the dwindling pile on the crowded picnic table.

"She said you were going to do presents later for Westin, but I got him something he might like now. Especially since I can see him in the river." She lifted her hand to wave in response to Westin's wild, long-armed wave.

"Let me guess. Something for the water?"

"Yep. Oh, it's so good to be here. Remember all the lazy summer days we spent in this river?"

"I remember. There's no better way to beat the heat." He fell in stride beside her, taking the towel to carry for her.

She squinted her pretty eyes at him as if trying to figure him out and slid her sunglasses down onto her nose. "It was nice of your sisters to invite me."

"Hey, I invited you, too."

"I'm ignoring that fact."

"Why, don't you trust me?"

Now, how did she answer that tricky question? Cadence ducked it entirely. "The government seems to trust you enough. Speaking of which, you're walking pretty well. The swimming is helping?"

"Yeah. I've been adding weight training and am gonna add some biking."

"Good. Start coming to the morning

swims, will you? You don't need to avoid me. I'm not trying to change your life. I'm not trying to do anything."

"Yes, but you're doing it all the same."

Was it her imagination, or did he dip closer, as if he were tempted to press a kiss to her cheek? Automatically she turned toward him, her mouth softening, wanting this strong, good man's kiss.

And wishing she didn't want his kiss.

But Westin came splashing out of the river, his hair shaped to his head, dripping water. "Cadence, is that for me?"

"Hey, way to go on the manners, buddy."

Cadence laughed. "It is. I got it because you're such a great swimmer. Why don't you open it, so you can play with it?"

"Wow. Thank you!" Westin eagerly took the package despite various comments on his manners, but Cadence was glad to see him happy. He'd been splashing and wading along the sandy bank, and that was a good sign after what he'd been through. She'd chosen his gift accordingly.

"You're spoiling him," Ben whispered in her ear. "Which is good, because we don't spoil him enough."

"You're pretty lucky to have him. My sister and brother haven't married, and so I have no nieces or nephews. I have to compensate for my lack somehow."

"Sure, you can't fool me, Cadence."

His words were tender, his smile gentle, but she could feel him thinking *I know what you want.* A family of her own wasn't too much to ask, but she'd learned enough life lessons to know that all things happened—or didn't happen—in God's time.

"You've always had a soft heart," he said instead, surprising her.

Tears smarted in her eyes and she blinked hard, grateful for the dark shades that hid her emotions from his sharp gaze. Nobody knew her the way Ben did. She feared no man ever would. What had he said about true love? *There's only one of those in a lifetime, and I'd already missed the chance at mine.* Was it true? Had they missed their only chance?

Something told her they had.

"Cool!" Westin held up the kid-sized mask, snorkel and fins set. "Wow, this is awesome. Thanks, Cadence. Now I can be more like Uncle Ben! This is what you gotta wear, right, Uncle Ben?"

"Yep. That's like scuba gear. Let's get you fixed up, buddy. Hold up your foot."

Ben took a flipper and loosened the strap as he knelt. Westin stuck out his left leg, wobbled and grabbed his uncle's shoulder for support.

Cadence watched, aching in a way she didn't understand as the big man slipped the wide plastic fin onto his nephew's foot. He strapped it up and did the same for the other foot. Every movement Ben made was caring, and the sight of that caring made the ache within her swell into an unbearable pain.

He would make such a great dad. He'd talked about wanting kids. Wanting to love and be loved.

She had to look away, grateful that Rachel was hurrying across the lawn holding an insulated oversize cup. She had a reason to break away and swallowed hard. She made sure none of the poignant emotion of longing and emptiness showed on her face or in her voice.

"Iced tea with lots of sugar and lemon,"

Rachel announced as she handed over the cup. "The only way to drink it. Sweet and cold and tangy."

"I agree. Thanks, Rache."

"No problem. That sure is a neat gift. As you tricked him into having so much fun, he'll forget to be afraid?"

"Something like that."

"Excellent. He seemed to do okay in the pool. He'll get his face underwater and kick, but when he gets in the river, he just wades. He doesn't like the current tugging at him. It's what pulled him under that one time. It's hard to blame him."

"The fins will help, too. He'll have a stronger kick, in case he does get caught in the current. Most people drown because they either don't know what to do or panic. While I'm here, I'll work with him."

"That would be so great. Would you mind if I called you sometime and we could do dinner and a movie?"

"I'd like that." She had work friends and her softball teammates, but the truth was, it had been a long time since she'd had a good, close friend. A best friend. The kind she knew Rachel would be. There went her heart, aching again, because she knew what was valuable in this life. What truly mattered.

Ben. His hand settled on her shoulder, a claiming touch. A connection. One that stirred her soul. He was an amazing man. A good man. Strong and decent and caring. Brave and loyal and faithful. Like a greatest dream.

As she watched him escort his nephew through the dappled shade, she felt her hold on her heart slip. The wide-shouldered man ambled with a limp alongside the lean, rangy boy, so alike, the wind rippling through their nearly identical hair.

There goes the man I love, she thought, falling completely and forever in love with him.

Again.

The one man she couldn't have. The one man she knew would leave her. And still she loved him. Because nothing could dim the blinding love that filled her, body and soul.

"Cadence is incredible," Amy pulled him aside to whisper in his ear. "I never thought we could get Westin into the deeper water, not without scaring him."

"Oh, he's scared, but he's not about to admit it." Just like me. But I don't want to go there, Ben thought as he hopped off the old wooden planks and into the cool water. "Heath, you're sure you want to man the grill?"

"I'm going to officially be part of this family in less than three weeks, so I'd best step up to the duties required of the man of the house." Heath cracked a grin and, for a moment as he gazed at Amy and then at Westin, his love was obvious.

I can't help liking this guy, Ben thought grudgingly, because it was hard to trust any man with his sister. But Heath worked hard at the diner, in addition to studying for the state medical board exams. He treated Amy like a queen and Westin like his own son.

A brother couldn't ask for more, and because these ties on his heart were too much, too intimate, too uncomfortable, he had to quip, "I'm glad you're here to take over, Heath. That leaves me free to take off."

"Stop teasing!" Amy rolled onto her stomach on the beach blanket to reach for her glass of iced tea. "You'd better be here for my wedding, or I'll have to trouble Uncle Pete to give me away. Which reminds me—you have a tux fitting this week."

"I didn't agree to wear a monkey suit." He waded against the current that tugged at his ankles.

"You didn't agree not to, mister." Amy chuckled, the sound lighthearted above the gurgling rush of the river. The easy banter between them was something that had gone on for years, so why was he so troubled? Amy knew he was simply teasing her, the right of big brothers everywhere, and he did it to make her laugh.

Maybe he was troubled because if his leg kept rebounding as it had, and his upcoming appointment with an orthopedic specialist in L.A. went well, then he'd be flying back to Hurlburt Field as soon as he could get back to light duty. Which meant, after the wedding.

Duty. It was as simple as that, although it had never made him feel torn before. He believed what he did was important. He couldn't live his life any other way. He didn't know how to. But for Cadence…?

A knot settled in his gut and tightened.

"Way to go, Westin!" She sparkled like the sunlight, looking sleek in her suit, which she'd had on beneath her clothes. Her hair was plastered to her head and billowed out in the water around her shoulders where she waded next to Westin. She held him buoyant in the water by the back band of his swimming trunks.

It looked as if the kid was getting the hang of it. He stretched out fully on his stomach and started paddling, facedown. The snorkel stuck up, so he could breathe easily, and the fins slapped and splashed inexpertly, but that would change with time.

Westin popped upright, spitting out his mouthpiece, which was well attached to the goggles and nosepiece. His smile was wide and confident. "I did it! The current didn't suck me in!"

"The fins help. And what do you do if you do get sucked away?"

"Swim like this." He made a diagonal

slice with his arm to the opposite bank. "Even if it's real far away?"

"Yep. You want to see how it works? Even a girl can do it."

"You can do it?"

"Sure. You stay right here, okay?" She waited until he'd nodded and his wide eyes told her he wasn't interested in sneaking out into the deeper water after her. Besides, Ben was striding closer to his nephew through the water, the river parting at his thighs. He nodded to her, indicating he'd look after Westin.

Good. She tried to keep her adoration for Ben to a minimum as she flashed him a grin.

While Westin watched, growing paler, she stretched out into an easy crawl stroke. Then she scissored as the wide river lulled her into the middle where the current twisted in on itself, moving swiftly and silently. It was strong, although the mighty river was at its laziest on this side of town. And there were no rapids and undertows that could foil even the strongest swimmers.

When she looked over her shoulder toward shore, treading water in the mighty current, she saw Westin sneak his hand into his uncle's. Side by side they stood watching her, but it was the man she could not look away from. The man who had her heart.

He always had.

He always would.

She didn't see the danger until it was too late. Until something clamped around her ankle, held on hard and yanked her down into the deep water.

Chapter Twelve

One moment Cadence had been staring directly into his soul, and the next she'd disappeared beneath the reflective surface. Too fast to have sunk on her own. A snag? A rope or some cable left by a boater?

Whatever it was, Ben barked an order to Westin to stay put and leaped deep into the water. He swam hard, keeping his eyes pinned to the exact spot where she'd disappeared.

Nothing.

She didn't surface, and his heart labored with utter terror as he tore up distance, counting the minutes. He had three minutes before oxygen began depleting in her blood. Four minutes until total brain death.

He'd been under the most extreme and stressful conditions on earth—combat, tribal warfare, urban fighting, water rescues assisting the coast guard during hurricanes. He'd been in a helicopter that was shot down behind enemy lines. No matter the crisis, he turned cold, deadly calm. Rational. Focused.

But this…never before had he fought so hard to stay in control of his panic.

The river was a wide deceptive stretch that had to be a good hundred feet wide, and the currents could have her anywhere. And the water was clean, but it was glacier runoff from the Rocky Mountain front. The river had sediment and dust, just enough to impede him from getting a good quick clear visual, if she was tangled up and trapped.

Then suddenly there was the sound of her merry laughter and the low-throated growl of a big dog's answer.

"Who on earth are you, fella?" she was saying, bobbing a good distance downstream. On the other side of the strongest current.

Beside her a big black-masked dog treaded water, giving her a toothy grin.

"Max!" Ben had never felt such an intense mix of relief and anger as he cut through the water. "What is wrong with you, you bad dog!"

"He was just playing." Cadence defended him as she rubbed the top of his waterlogged head. "At first I thought it was the Loch Ness monster, since I couldn't think of anything so powerful that lived in this river. No crocodiles. No giant anacondas. I've never heard of a bear stealing through the water."

"No dog biscuits for you," he told the rottweiler, who was more puppy than grown dog. Max was unashamed and unapologetic as he splashed over to try to lay a sloppy kiss on him. Ben gave him a gentle shove. "Back. Go. You tried to drown Cadence."

"He's okay. Although you came out to save me."

Save her? He hadn't realized it, but he knew now he'd die for her. He'd do anything to keep her safe. Anything to make her happy. It was a scary realization, but it was there all the same, growing stronger as Paige started scolding her dog from the faraway dock. Alex, his amazingly grown-up other nephew, waded out into the current and called his dog.

The beast gave a bark of either warning or apology and took off with great excitement, as if he hadn't done anything wrong at all.

"Sorry!" Alex called, cupping his hands to throw his voice across the water. "He and I were roughhousing earlier."

"He's a nice dog." Cadence seemed to truly mean it.

Ben still couldn't seem to catch his breath. All he saw was images of finding her too late. Hauling her out of the water, starting mouth-to-mouth and CPR and having her lifeless in his arms.

Images that haunted him from battle, since a lot of his combat work involved administering paramedic and lifesaving medical care in the field. He'd held a lot of dying soldiers, but to think he could have lost Cadence…his heart stopped.

"Don't scare me like that again," he rasped, not caring that the water was twenty feet deep. He didn't care if the entire family was watching. He hauled her against him, where she felt so right and familiar against his chest.

Thank You, God. She was warm and fragile and fit against him as if God had designed them to be together. He cupped the back of her head with his hand and gave thanks to the heavens above that she was safe.

"I was perfectly safe," she assured him. "The dog was only playing, and he didn't scare me. As soon as my head was underwater, I saw him and his laughing eyes and I knew he was only playing. He's strong, though."

"He's still a puppy and doesn't have the best sense yet." Ben rolled his eyes. "Alex got him a year ago last Christmas. Our cousin Kirby and her husband have a rott, and this is one of his puppies. I helped Alex pick him out."

"You only come home for Christmas?"

"When they let me. Otherwise I'm fast roping from helicopters. Doing a night jump at high altitudes. Maybe sleeping dug into a sand dune with MREs to comfort me."

"You make it sound so luxurious."

"I miss it." He looked away, wishing he didn't have to think about that. How much he'd give up to get back to his squad. To do what he loved best. Except his duty was far away across an ocean and on another continent and Cadence was in his arms, more of a risk to his heart than enemy fire at close range.

"Max!" a chorus of voices belted out, drawing Cadence's attention away from him—and in the nick of time, before he did something foolish and final, something he couldn't take back. He was not about to play with Cadence's heart. Or his own. He loved her too much. He would love her forever. But what would she do if she knew that?

Run. And who would blame her?

"Max!" More scolds rose on the pleasant breeze, echoing across the water and in the tree canopies.

The big dog did another shake, spraying cold river water and dog hair everywhere. Paige, apparently having enough of the rambunctious puppy, grabbed him by his collar and hauled him away from the loungers, but not roughly. When she thought no one was looking, she knelt and gave the big guy a hug. That was his

Paige—gentle hearted and didn't want anyone to know it.

"I would love a dog like that," Cadence was saying, swimming away from him now, the dangerous moment between them safely past.

Thank goodness for small blessings.

"Yeah," he agreed about the dog, "but I'm not home enough."

"Me, either."

"C'mon, let's swim in. Amy's waving to us. Heath is gone. Probably starting the barbecue."

"I made a promise to Westin. He's still watching." As if she needed to get away from him, she took off for the shore where a thick growth of cottonwoods, alder and maple shaded the water and left no bank. She didn't seem to care as she stroked silently, putting distance between them.

Probably wise, he told himself. But he couldn't stop the pang of regret as he headed for the opposite shore.

It was a beautiful evening, Cadence thought, drawing to a stop at Ben's side next to her car. She so didn't want it to end.

The barbecued meal had been delicious,
Westin had had fun opening his gifts and
the conversation and family banter over
dessert had warmed her from the inside
out.

Now it was over.

Larks and chickadees flitted by to hang
on tree limbs or the top rails of the fence.
Rachel's horse lifted his big head to watch
them, as if in hope they had something for
him to eat. Deciding not, he returned to his
grazing.

As if threatening to take over entirely,
the long shadows of twilight fell across the
driveway and onto the newly graveled
road. Overhead the big moon glowed
weakly in a cloud-streaked sky and rain
scented the air, although there was no sign
of it overhead.

Life was like that, too. Clear sailing,
blue skies and then a sudden change in the
wind. Disaster.

And she was looking disaster in the face:
Ben. It was as if she could feel his presence
like the breath in her lungs. Like the beat
of her own heart. How was it that he stood
so tall in her view? No matter what hap-

pened in her life, or what had happened between them, he was a big, awesome man.
The only one who mattered.

As if sensing her thoughts, he turned to
face her, his hands caressing in a slow
sweep from her shoulder along her arms to
her fingertips. Everything within her twinkled like the first stars of the night. Hesi-
tant. Illuminating.

I love you so much, Ben McKaslin. It
was undeniable. As sweet as the summer
evening. And it moved through her soul
like the gentle breezes, stirring up everything within her, as if making her new.

Hope colored her like the sunset on the
clouds, bright and stunning, and impossible to ignore. What was happening to her?
Why was she being carried away like this?

*Please, Lord, don't let me make a mis-
take. Please don't let me love this man,*
she prayed, even though it was too late.

Ben. He smiled at her and her heart
stopped. He cupped her face with his big
hands, so close she could see the hazel-
green threads in his dark irises and the character lines drawn into the corners of his eyes.

"I'm still reeling from watching you go

under in that river. Don't ever do that to me again." Tenderness and love filled those words.

See how impossible it was to resist him? she thought. Her willpower was not enough. Nor were her lessons learned the hard way. She felt as she had in the river when Max had her by the ankle, swiftly being pulled under—no control, too little air and the sudden surprise of it.

His lips slanted over hers, hovering for one brief moment. She trembled, feeling her heart unwillingly open a little bit more. Vulnerable, she waited, afraid of letting him into the room of her heart. Afraid not to, because she did not want to miss this chance to know love. Real love. For however how briefly it might last.

He leaned in, closing the scant inch separating their waiting lips. The first brush of his kiss was like warmed velvet against hers. The sweetest caress. Her spirit sighed. The second brush of his kiss was not so brief, but ardent and tender. When he released her, she stumbled, overcome.

True love. There it was. In her heart. In her hopes. In his kiss.

"I'm leaving Monday to see a specialist in Los Angeles." Like the gentleman he was, he opened her car door for her.

She was hardly aware of settling behind the wheel, looking up at him through the frame of her open window. "How long will you be gone?"

"About a week. I've got some physical therapists I want to consult, too. I'm not sure how long it'll take." Ben shrugged, the gray knit of his T-shirt clinging to the muscled curves of his hard shoulders. "But I'll be back in plenty of time for Amy's wedding. I'll see you there?"

She nodded, when everything within her screamed at her to say no. Today had been too much. She was already impossibly in love with him. She should keep her distance, but she didn't want to. She wanted to spend as much time with Ben as she could before he returned to active duty. If there was a possibility for more...

No, don't even think that. She put a halt to those thoughts. There was no way she could begin to set herself up like that. Ben had his duty. She had her teaching.

While she could teach anywhere, especially in Florida, that didn't mean Ben wanted to take her there. While he was an incredible man, he had been clear. He wasn't ready to settle down. And in truth she'd had enough men walking away from her. Letting her down. This time she would let Ben go the way he needed to. And she'd do it with dignity. It was the right thing, but not the easy choice.

"Have a safe trip," she said. "I'll see you at the wedding."

"Count on it."

See? He was already moving away from her. He stood with his weight evenly balanced. The red puckered scars from his injury and surgeries remained, a reminder of why he'd come home. And why he would leave.

Choices. That's what a person's life came down to. Choices made either by your own will or by God's guiding hand. But choices all the same, she thought as she started the car and buckled her seat belt.

God had brought them together. Why? Certainly being with Ben had healed the past between them. Even softened the blow of Tom's abandonment. Maybe that was all He'd intended.

And that meant it was enough.

Giving the worry up to the Lord, Cadence backed out, waved to Ben and drove away. She refused to watch the solitary figure in the center of the rearview mirror, the one who was watching her go.

And letting her.

Rachel startled him by laying a hand on his arm. "Things are going pretty well between you and Cadence, huh?"

He swallowed, his jaw tightening until his molars hurt. No. Things were not going well at all. "What did you see?"

"Enough. She's a sweetheart and I never understood why you didn't grab her and never let her go."

"I was eighteen. What did I know?"

"Exactly. Except you're not eighteen now. And a little wiser?"

He didn't feel any wiser.

The gelding nickered, spotting his mistress, and Rachel loped the few yards to the board fence. Nuzzling her horse seemed to occupy her.

Ben turned away in relief. The only sign of Cadence's presence was the faint cloud of dust in the air, settling now and fading. Soon it would be gone, and the evening would be as if she'd never been here. The evening chores would still need to be done, just like always. Nothing appeared different, which absolutely shocked him.

Because everything had changed.

Life-altering moments were like that. He'd spent nearly fifteen years hoofin' it as a Special Forces soldier. That meant he didn't wait for a war to happen. He'd been waging it every day. Rescuing pilots, diplomats, providing protection or medical aid in hot zones wherever he was needed.

When a soldier was shot, when a team buddy died, when a victim of tribal warfare couldn't be saved, it was as if the world could never be right again. Something tragic and profound ought to have an impact on the fabric of the world. But time kept marching on, day turned to night and the globe kept right on spinning.

Kissing Cadence was one of those moments. It stuck with him, the surge of affection he could not hold back. The widening of her eyes as he'd drawn closer. The sensation of being lost in those big blue eyes. It had been as if a current more powerful than the river's had seized him and his lips had covered hers.

Perfection. She was his perfect match. He didn't need a sign from heaven to know it. He felt it, for the answer was in his soul. True love didn't die or fade or diminish, not with time or mistakes or regret. It remained like a stubborn candle that would not let cold winds or dark nights destroy it.

But true love was only a single flame.

"Hey, I'm gonna take Nugget for a run. Will you be all right?"

Would he be? He didn't know. "Yeah. Sure. I'm just gonna catch the rest of the baseball game."

Rachel had climbed through the fence and was in the process of hopping onto the horse's bare back. The sleek golden animal stood patiently while Rachel settled onto his broad back. His affection was obvious as he lapped at her knee, as if glad to be with her.

With a fistful of mane she leaned forward to whisper in his ear, and the great beast took off, loping through the tall seed-heavy grasses and wildflowers.

"Uncle Ben! Uncle Ben!" Westin burst through the screen door with a bang and pounded toward him. In one hand he clutched the snorkeling gear Cadence had gotten him and in the other, the latest video game he'd wanted. "Is it okay if we take the tent home? Please? Please?"

"Sure, buddy. You know where it is. Don't forget your sleeping bag, too."

"Yeah! This is gonna be so cool! Heath knows gobs about camping, too. He's gonna show me how to build a campfire with sticks and we're gonna make our own s'mores right there!"

The kid was so excited. Happy. That's the way he ought to be. It was a big event, getting a new dad. Heath was a good man. He'd be a great father. That's what every kid deserved.

Ben couldn't explain why his throat seized up, but he was glad for his nephew. And grateful that there would be a good strong man in his life to help him grow up.

Lord knew Ben wouldn't be around much, and it cut deep.

Life. It seemed to be what other people got to live.

"Thanks, Uncle Ben!" Westin tromped off, leaving the door to bang shut behind him.

What was with him? When he'd first driven up after that long exhausting trek from Florida, it had been with trepidation. He hadn't wanted to be here. The memories, the relationships, the ties, they just ate at him—not because he didn't care, but because he cared too much.

His parents were here, their memories. Memories of Mom standing at the front door, shading her eyes to check first on his whereabouts and then on her horses. Of barbecue suppers on the back patio with his sisters yakking up a storm and Dad's cigar smoke mixing with the scent of charred meat, lighter fluid and briquettes.

Of the warm mantle of sunlight and togetherness and family. Of his believing that life would always be like this. That he'd have his parents forever. He'd always have a home and family.

But life had shown him something different. It had been so long ago, the pain of their loss had faded. But it wasn't the past sorrow that hurt him, he realized as he caught a glimpse of Rachel and Nugget at the pasture's edge, racing the wind.

It was the ties on his heart that hurt. Because he didn't want them. He didn't want to trust in anything so fleeting and fragile.

Life was fleeting. Love was something you couldn't place your hopes on. Things happened, life changed and suddenly there was no home, no family and no loved ones.

All he could do was his job, protecting them so his sisters and nephews could sleep safely at night. He made a difference.

It used to be enough.

Chapter Thirteen

"I practiced really hard over the weekend," Ashley announced with the enthusiasm of a teenager as she perched a few yards from the end of the platform. "I did handstands until my mom said I had to stop."

"Excellent. Then let's see it. I'll spot you."

Cadence didn't need to check the edge of the platform. She knew the feel of it by heart, backing up to the edge where the diving pool waited, nearly flawless in the late-afternoon quiet.

A few swim team members had come early, and their coach's low murmur became indistinguishable in the giant hush of the building. She always felt a thrill being so high and knowing how wondrous it was to fall into the waiting water.

"Take your time," she advised. Hours of practice at home and in the gym were different than on the platform. "I'm here when you're ready."

"Okay. I can do this," Ashley muttered more to herself, and stared hard at the textured surface, where she would place her hands.

Cadence waited patiently while the girl bent. She placed a hand on the training harness, holding her steady. "Get your balance," she reminded the girl.

Ashley answered by wobbling, struggling to find her center of balance. Concentrating so hard, Cadence knew, there was nothing else for her but the rough texture of the platform, the fight of strength and balance and the total calm of imagining the sequence of the coming dive.

Ashley was serious as she became as solid as a world-class diver on the edge of the platform, spotting through her hands to the water below. She tensed and sprang. Cadence made certain Ashley cleared the dangerous edge of the platform before she plunged straight down in a graceful, perfect arch. Hardly a splash marred the surface of the water.

Ashley surfaced. "That was awesome! Oh, I gotta do it again."

Ah, the love of diving. It was a blessing on a day like this. She was missing Ben. Not that she wanted to admit how deeply he'd crept into her heart. She swore her lips still remembered the loving sweetness of his kiss.

Don't think about him, Cadence. Because if she thought about him, it was as if she were missing a chunk of her heart.

"Ah, Miss Chapman?"

A girl's voice drew her attention. There on the deck in front of the women's locker rooms was a teenager in cover-ups, looking uncertain as she clutched her towel. She chewed on her bottom lip, showing a hint of braces on her teeth.

Of course—her new student. "Hi, Jennifer. Go ahead and shower up, then pick a lane and swim a few laps to warm up. I'll be with you in a few minutes."

"Okay. Thank you." Jennifer padded away as a woman who must have been her mom took a seat in the empty bleachers overhead.

Out of breath, Ashley lurched up the ladder. "I can't believe I didn't even wobble that time. I can do it again. I know I can."

As she spotted Ashley's last few dives, Cadence fought to keep her thoughts on her job. But the instant she waved goodbye to Ashley, her mind seemed to go into overdrive. Images of Ben in the river, when he'd thought she was drowning, swimming as if his life depended on it, his face intense. Fierce. Determined. It still stunned her. No one—ever—had radiated that level of concern for her.

Ben cradling her face and gazing into her eyes as if he wanted to spend eternity with her. And his kiss, so very tender.

Ben, his reflection in her rearview mirror, soldier straight as she drove away.

Sure, her heart was missing him, but she had to get used to it. Soon he would be leaving for good. She had to stop caring for him right now. Right here. It was the sensible thing to do. It was simple self-preservation.

Because if not seeing Ben for a week

hurt this much, think of how it would be for the rest of her life.

Crouched in an uncomfortable chair in the specialist's packed waiting room, Ben cradled the pocket-size cell phone in his hand. It was Rachel's. In case he wanted to call home or Cadence, she'd said with a knowing wink. Well, he'd call home when he knew the final opinion on his leg and he'd call Cadence when he got up the courage.

Her number had been mysteriously programmed into the phone—proof that Rachel had been scheming in a nice way—and he was looking at that number on the display, which he'd pulled up. All he had to do was hit the dial button and the phone would connect and he could hear her voice. Talk to her.

And then what? He punched off the power button and slid the phone into his pocket. It wasn't as if they had a future. It wasn't as if he could ask her to give up everything, marry him and move to Florida. Where she'd be alone for most of the year worrying about what he was doing, if he was safe. It wasn't as if that was even a remote possibility. Right?

He checked his watch—four-thirty. He'd been waiting for a one-o'clock appointment. Not a patient man, he forced himself to sit there and grab another sports magazine. It was last month's, but he snapped it open anyway. For the billionth time the receptionist started explaining to the latest arrival that the doctor had been called to emergency surgery and if she wished to wait…

Yeah, he was about finished with waiting, but he knew what the base docs had to say. He'd consulted his hometown doc, who'd done some research and come up with this guy. He'd better be worth the wait, Ben thought as he flipped through pages, the phone a weight in his pocket he forced himself to ignore.

Cadence grabbed her duffel and the plastic sack of groceries she'd picked up on the way home. She had two more days until payday, and her funds were pretty thin. It was a good thing she loved mac and cheese. It was easy, quick and on sale, the perfect combination. Plus, she'd been able to squeeze in a pint of her favorite ice cream without breaking her budget.

Another wildfire outside the city had gained a hold in the foothills and the city was rank with smoke. Her eyes stung and her lungs felt scratchy as she hurried the short distance from her assigned parking spot to her front door.

The sinking sun bled across the hazy sky, an eerie sight, and she was glad to get out of the heat and smoke and into the quiet of her hot town house. She deposited the bags on the table and went straight to the thermostat. A few degrees made the unit kick on and wheeze out some cooler air.

Alone, she grabbed the TV remote, clicked on the local news. While it droned in the background, she listened with half an ear as she put the milk and ice cream away. Through the little window over the sink she saw the neighbors two units down on their way from their car to their door. The married couple walked with their little boy between them. His dark hair was askew and he had blue finger paint streaked across his white shirt. He tromped along with supreme confidence between the two people who loved him most.

Her heart broke with want. Her kitchen echoed with her movements as she slid a blue box onto the counter and put the others away in the small pantry. She had so many blessings, ones she truly treasured, and she shouldn't be looking to the ones she didn't have. No good could ever come from that.

But she wished, how she wished, that Ben would call. True love—how she ached for it in her life. And, it seemed, it had passed her by again.

She listened for the phone, as she'd done every evening since he'd left town. Hoping. Of course he was busy. He was visiting friends, seeing health care providers and maybe even seeing a baseball game. She was glad for him that he got to enjoy himself before he went back to the war.

The national network news was on, showing a harsh, arid-looking shot of urban fighting. Of American soldiers who'd been attacked. Listing the names of the two marines who'd died.

Thank You, God, for men like Ben. She tucked her sadness aside, and when she sat down to her plate of creamy mac and cheese and a favorite syndicated rerun on TV, she bowed her head for grace, and wound up praying for Ben. *Please, Father, let him get good news about his injury. Let him return to the job he loves.*

The phone remained silent all evening. And for the next two evenings after that. It seemed God might have answered her prayer after all.

"What do you mean, you agree?" After waiting another day and two hours today to be squeezed in for a five-minute appointment, Ben had fought with frustration all morning, but now...now it was worth it. "You think I can return to active duty?"

"Not today, dude." One of the most respected orthopedic surgeons on the West Coast looked as if he ought to be out on the beach catching a wave instead of peering at MRI film. "It's never gonna be one hundred percent, but who is? I've got some names of some totally cool rehab therapists. I don't know what you get in the military, but I promise you, dude, these ladies are world-class. They know how to get results. Come back and see me if you run into trouble."

"I can't thank you enough."

"Hey, you hung in there waitin' for me." The renowned specialist loped off, calling for his nurse.

The efficient woman came with the promised therapists' names, a prescription and samples of an anti-inflammatory drug. Unbelievably, Ben was on his way.

He felt ten times lighter as he waded through the waiting room, which was still packed. As soon as he was outside, it was all he could do not to shout, "Hoo-yah" and give his colonel a call. But first he grabbed the phone, scrolled through the programmed numbers and hit the button. It rang four times before an answering machine picked up.

"Hi, I can't take your call right now." The sound of Cadence's voice, cheerful and resonant, made his throat tighten. The places in him that filled with light when he was around her stung with emptiness.

"Please leave your number so I know you've called."

He disconnected before the beep.

I miss her so much. His entire spirit ached with longing he could no longer deny. He wanted to deny it, but he couldn't. He was a man, a soldier, a PJ. There wasn't anything he couldn't do if he tried hard enough.

But the agony that welled up from his soul at the sound of her voice and the disappointment of not being able to talk to her defeated him. He had to fight down the urge to race home, knock on her door, pull her into his arms and hold her as tight as he could as long as he could. Forever. And never let her go.

Overwhelmed, he snapped off the phone. As if he could say that to her. He wanted what he couldn't have. He didn't even know if she felt this for him. What was it she'd said about love? True love has to go both ways for it to work, or something like that.

Life hadn't been this complicated before. He'd never wanted anything so much. Just Cadence. He felt weak with it. Strong with it. Confused. He'd never felt so mixed up and torn up and sure at the same time.

He didn't only want to see Cadence the instant he stepped foot on Montana soil. He wanted her to have and to hold for the rest of his life.

And there was no way he was going to be able to have that.

Ben's coming home today.

For the ten billionth time Cadence shoved that thought out of her mind as she climbed out of the diving pool. It was payday. She had a bunch of errands to do. A stop at the bank. A few bills to pay. Groceries—which meant something other than mac and cheese tonight. And she had to do her laundry. She'd run completely out of towels. Those were the things she ought to be thinking about instead.

But what was the next thought that filled her head? Ben's coming home today.

Stop! she commanded, mentally shaking her head. She was setting herself up for absolute devastation. There was no reason to think Ben was going to rush right over here from the airport, wrap her in his arms and confess his undying love to her. He'd gone to seek second opinions on his recovering injury. He had plans and a future, and it wouldn't be here in Montana with her.

What had he said to her the day he'd brought dinner to her house? *Not many men with my job marry. I watched buddy after buddy of mine bail out of the PJs. I had to make a choice.*

That was answer enough. She padded past the platforms and hopped onto the springboard, loving the spring and bounce of it beneath her feet. She trusted it like an old friend as she hopped around on the edge, relaxing her muscles as the board sprang beneath her weight, settling.

She leaped, soaring up toward the rafters, stretching for her toes in a pike position and then reaching back as the air rushed against her face, her fingers grabbing the mirrored surface. The cool rush of water as she slid beneath it with not a splash to be heard.

With the odd buoyant sounds of the water in her ears, she frog kicked toward the ladder. And where did her mind go the instant she wasn't diving? Ben. Why? She knew he wasn't looking for a wife. He wasn't husband material. He never had been. He'd broken her heart over that once.

He would do it again. He wouldn't mean to. He wouldn't want to. But he wasn't a settling-down type, or he would have settled. And look at her life—she had financial problems, she had debts to pay and she had built a full roster of diving students who relied on her. She was about as tied down as a single woman without kids could be.

What she needed was to be realistic. Ben was home, probably on his way to his sister's house. She prayed he'd received good news. That meant she might not see him before the wedding. After all, why would their paths cross before that? Westin was finished with his lessons—he was going to be going on the honeymoon with Amy and Heath. A family trip to Walt Disney World and a two-week cruise after that. He'd be back in time for the fall session that would begin with the start of public school.

She had to be prepared for Ben to leave, she thought as she bolted out of the water.

She had to keep him from breaking her heart. She'd let him too far into her heart already, and she dreaded knowing that she would feel the devastation of his rejection.

"Hey, is that a way to greet a guy?"

Ben? She spun at the sound of his voice, so shocked to see him she could only stare. It wasn't her imagination conjuring him up. It was really him, standing there in jeans and a plain T-shirt that made him look all man. She wanted to run to him. She wanted to wrap her arms around him and hold him forever. To give him all the love that shone in her heart.

Hadn't she just vowed to keep her dignity? To protect her heart and not go handing it over to the tough guy who would never be hers? But she wanted him to be.

Dripping, she took a steadying breath. She was glad she had, once she took in the details—of his set jaw, his shoulders squared, his legs planted. A confrontational look.

He didn't seem comfortable or happy to be here at all. And even if her spirit filled with an amazing brightness when she saw him, she was not blind to the fact that he was frowning at her. So why had he come?

Confused, she fisted her hands, not knowing what else to do. He just stood there, staring at her, looking like a soldier ready for war.

Hadn't it gone well in California? She wanted to comfort him. To say the right words to soothe. Bad news from the doctor had to be a bitter disappointment. But if she did try to comfort him, then anything she did or said would involve her heart. It would make her feelings clear to him, while he'd been perfectly clear with her all along. He wanted to be friendly, not friends. He wanted to return to active duty. What else could she do?

He could have been stone, as motionless as he was.

Then she understood. He'd come to say goodbye. The realization rocked through her like a punch to her jaw. She wobbled, fighting for balance and composure. She hadn't expected to end this with him so soon. And to have him here looking as if he'd rather be anywhere else.

So she'd been the only one in love. Again, she thought, feeling the pain of it hit her heart. Ben had hurt her. After all.

"I, uh, saw you dive." He motioned toward the springboard that was still faintly quivering. "Either that looks better in person than it did on TV, or you're doing this a lot better than you did in the Olympics."

"Everything gets better with practice." She shrugged. Diving was a passion, no different to her than sports or needlepoint or crossword puzzles to other people. It was how she relaxed, how she had fun, how she coped. "I'm sorry. Was it bad news?"

"Bad news? No. Why do you say that?" His eyebrows drew down, his frown deepened. He looked more fierce than ever. "No, the doc said the bone's coming along. I consulted some rehab specialists who work with world-class athletes, so they know about coming back from injuries, and I have a real good plan to get back to pass the qualifying tests. I need to call my commander, but it looks like I'm going back."

"Congratulations." Remember your vow, she told herself as she made her feet step forward and carry her across the deck. "You don't look so happy about it."

"I am. I'm just impatient." A muscle ticked in his jaw. "It'll take a good part of the next year before I'm fully back in shape."

Hope leaped into her heart. Against all common sense, against her will, against every ounce of dignity she had, there it was, hoping against hope that if he stayed for a while, they could become more than friends. And then all the love she carried for him in her heart would—

"I'm heading back to Florida right after Amy's wedding." His words blew apart her hopes like an unpinned grenade. "I've got to get the go-ahead from my commander, but I can get back to work. Probably training new recruits to the program right out of boot camp, and I'll work on my leg otherwise. Probably be back in the desert by this time next year. Maybe sooner."

"That's wonderful news for you, Ben." She put the closest thing she could manage to a smile on her face, willing down the pain, refusing to let him see the heartbreak building. She blinked hard. Swallowed harder. Let air into her lungs. After all, lost hopes weren't fatal. She'd learned that the hard way, too. "It's everything we've been praying for."

"Yep."

Ben took a step back. He should ask her flat out how she felt about him. Just ask her. But she seemed pretty reserved about his news. It wasn't what he had been picturing when he'd been crammed in that tin can of a plane. She stayed back, as if she didn't want to get close to him. Was it because she'd figured out that whatever they had going between them was over? He would be going back. Or was it because he was the only one in love?

Just ask her. But the tightness in his chest increased. He was afraid. What if she said she wasn't in love with him? She'd given him no indication that she was. He didn't want to make a fool of himself. What if he'd blown any chances of being with her all those years ago? He'd been a kid, wet behind the ears and thinking he knew everything.

He'd been wrong, and he'd hurt her. What if she was never going to trust him with her heart again? He couldn't blame her. Simply seeing her filled his soul with an agonizing brightness.

"I'm glad you dropped by to tell me." She smiled, genuinely this time, but the rest of her remained tensed. Cool. "I know how important your job is. It's a passion and a calling, and sometimes those things require sacrifices."

"They do."

So she did understand. Maybe that's why she understood him so well, because she had a job she loved, too. She had a good thing here. She didn't make a lot of money, but then, neither did he.

Money didn't matter as much as most things—family, loved ones, job satisfaction. He was a PJ, one of the toughest Special Forces soldiers the military trained, and he had to come half a world away to Montana to face the toughest challenge— one of his heart.

And he was failing. He couldn't say the words *Marry me,* because he already knew the answer. Cadence wouldn't give up her life to move to Florida. She was no longer his one true love.

He'd blown it. It was as clear as day. That's why she stood as stiff as stone looking at him from across the pool deck. She hadn't run into his arms. She hadn't missed him. She'd not even commented on the kiss he'd impulsively given her before he left.

"You must be so happy to be going back."

Was it his imagination, or was her bottom lip trembling? Or was it simply his hope that this was killing her on the inside, the way it was killing him? I want to choose you, he thought, feeling his heart begin to crack into pieces. Somehow he managed to speak past the tight ache in his throat. "Ecstatic."

"You don't look happy."

"I'm just in a lot of pain." Emotional pain. The only thing relationships brought him. He wasn't good at them. He couldn't even tell Cadence, whom he loved without end, that he loved her. That he wanted her. He didn't know what to do with the immeasurable love he felt for her.

There was no way he could make her feel the same way.

Agony twisted in his chest, emotions coiling up so tight, he couldn't begin to figure out what they were. All he knew was that he needed her. He loved her so much, he was pretty sure that nothing—not even his job—mattered more.

"You'll have to give me your e-mail address, so we can write." She was no longer straining to smile. No longer moving in his direction. She'd stopped, and now she was backing up. "So we can keep in touch. If you want."

"Uh…yeah." It occurred to him in that moment that she was letting him go, her choice made.

And he had to make his. "I'll see you at the wedding, then? Or have you changed your mind?"

"I'll probably go," she said quietly, compressing her lips together instead of showing any emotion.

Please, he begged her, give me a sign. Do you want me? Will you trust me with your heart?

But nothing.

So he turned and walked away. There was nothing else he could do.

Chapter Fourteen

Lord, I don't know how I can go to the wedding. Cadence closed her devotional and set the small book on her kitchen table beside her Bible. While she was happy for Amy and Westin, for this marriage seemed to be a true blessing to their lives, she was not looking forward to seeing Ben. To pretending she didn't feel this endless love for him.

It would be simple not to go. She could make excuses, and stay away from the wedding. Her heart had been battered enough. She could send the gift. Surely Amy would understand.

But it wouldn't be right, her conscience reminded her. It would be cowardly.

Yeah, but it sure would be easier if she didn't see Ben one more time. Seeing him would only make her wish, and she'd had enough lost dreams to know that nothing was going to come from this one.

It was better to let him go now. To write him out of her life. To stop thinking about him. Stop wishing for him. Stop—somehow—the love from growing ever bigger and more consuming in her soul. That would be the sensible and practical thing to do. It was self-preservation.

But missing the wedding was not the right thing to do. Rachel had promised to save her a seat in the church. The McKaslins had once been like family to her. How could she not help them celebrate the blessing of true love in Amy's life?

It was not an easy thing getting ready for the wedding. She wore her best summer sundress, a floral pattern with straps that crisscrossed her back and a ruffled full skirt that shivered around her when she walked. She'd added matching strappy sandals and a strand of fake pearls at her throat.

She took the time to French braid her hair, although she was running a bit late.

The less time spent waiting in the church for the ceremony to start, the less time to see Ben, to think about Ben and to try to hold back the tides of her heart.

At ten minutes past noon she grabbed her purse, keys and the carefully wrapped gift and locked the front door behind her. The wildfire had been curbed in the past few days so that the haze was nearly gone from the air, although the wind still stung of smoke. She climbed into her car and headed out of the city.

The fertile mountain river valley rolled out before her, gorgeous in the midday sun. The awesome peaks of the Rocky Mountains jutted up from the valley floor, growing closer and rising higher as she followed the highway west and took the exit to the small town of Manhattan.

Memories rolled by her. Of being six years old and riding to the drive-in for ice cream on her rusty pink bike with the training wheels Mom had picked up at the secondhand store. The small forgotten trailer park beyond the alley behind the grocery store where she'd lived with her family in a fourteen-foot trailer when her dad was out of work for a year.

The main street, polished and renewed with new shops and restaurants—the town benefiting from the building boom in Bozeman—seemed not so changed. Kids still rode their ponies to town. Boys on bikes raced down the sidewalk. Families picnicked in the town's central park. A part of her would always be the little country girl who'd grown up here.

The church was packed. It was also beautiful. Pale pink ribbons draped the bouquets at the ends of the aisles. Pink and white roses were everywhere and the sweet fragrance scented the air.

A tall teenage boy in a tux, whom she recognized as Paige's son, took her gift and pointed out the family area in the front. She stood on tiptoe, trying to see if there was possibly any room for her. There didn't look to be, and in truth, she prayed there wasn't. The farther away she was from Ben, the better.

But then Rachel popped up, hurrying toward her in a beautiful pink dress and matching heels, and gave her a welcoming hug. "Oh, I was so worried you wouldn't come! Follow me."

Negotiating the aisle wasn't easy, for attendees were still sitting down, kids were darting down the aisle and folks stood in groups, talking with friends, loved ones and neighbors. Snippets of conversation, from the morning's rise in wheat prices to comments on the flowers, rose above the soft classical organ music being played in the front of the modest, old-fashioned church. Bach, she thought, but she wasn't sure.

Rachel led the way to the front pews, twisting around to talk as they went. "I told Ben I'd keep an eye out for you. He's giving Amy away, you know. It's a tough job for him, because he's a big softie underneath all the tough-guy stuff and it's hard giving up a sister."

"They will still be living in town, won't they?"

"Oh, sure. There's a big argument going on between us." She rolled her eyes, the gesture indicating it wasn't such a serious disagreement. "I say she and Heath and Westin ought to have the family home, where I'm living. I love the seclusion, but really, I don't need all that space, not when, after today, it will be the three of them squished into Amy's little trailer." She darted into the front row. "I say they should take the house—excuse me, Paige—and I'd be as happy as could be in the snug little trailer, but Amy's too stubborn."

"Independent," Paige corrected with a wink. "Hi, Cadence. Have you seen Ben yet?"

She shook her head, touched by the warm welcome as Paige stood to hug her, too. "I just arrived."

"I think he was trying to avoid you earlier. You know men and weddings. But you're his date—"

"Not really. Not officially."

"Why, of course you are." Rachel spoke up, determined on her brother's behalf. "He's just asked us to look after you until he can join us. Oh, look, they're going to start."

"Aren't you a bridesmaid, in that lovely dress?"

"Oh, no. Amy had a better idea, and we

all loved it so much." Rachel beamed. "You wait and see."

The music changed. The soft sonorous chords of the wedding march brought the guests to their feet. The minister settled behind the altar. The sun chose that moment to beam more brightly through the tall stained-glass windows, casting jeweled light like a blessing.

From the vestibule, two tuxedoed figures flanked Amy, petite and beautiful in a princess's gown of white. She had one gloved hand on her little son's arm and the other on her brother's.

Ben. Cadence's heart wrenched so hard, it brought tears to her eyes. Let everyone think she was moved by happiness for Amy. It was true. She was deeply glad that Amy had found a forever kind of love in the solemn man waiting for her at the altar. He seemed to stand strong with a great love for her.

When the minister asked, "Who gives this woman in marriage?" Heath was already reaching for her, reverent and loving.

"We do," Ben and Westin answered together.

Amy stepped forward, her hand in Heath's, and the music was replaced by silence. No accompaniment was necessary as the couple gazed into each other's eyes. True love.

It was a reason to rejoice. Cadence swiped at the corners of her eyes, delicately trying to hide the dampness because she wanted her own happy ending. She would be content that Amy had found hers. Sometimes true love found a way even in this complicated world.

Ben made his way to the family pew. "Excuse me," he whispered to his sisters, but they refused to budge.

"Move on, bud," Rachel whispered, apparently unsympathetic to her brother's need to sit somewhere other than the space at Cadence's left-hand side.

Cadence tried not to let it bother her. She moved down so Ben could sit next to Rachel, and earned Ben's questioning look. But the minister had started to speak, so he took the space on the pew, his iron-hard thigh pressing against hers. His shoulder was like steel.

There was no way to ignore the fact that she was so close and yet so distant from him.

"I'm glad you came." Ben leaned close to speak against her ear.

He was? Well, then they were still friends after all. Was it all they could ever be? Her heart yearned for him. Her soul was filled with his presence. It was impossible not to fall even more in love with this wonderful, good man in his black tux, solemn and faithful as he bowed his head in prayer.

Beside him, she did the same, determined to keep her sorrow tucked away. She'd been fine all these years without Ben. She'd be fine for the rest of the years to come without him in her life. Think of all the good reasons God had brought them together again. To heal them both of regrets. To help Westin—Amy might not have started his swimming lessons so soon if Cadence's path hadn't crossed Ben's.

And she would never have gotten to know for sure—for absolute sure—that good men did exist. She'd been disillusioned through her experiences, it was true—her fiancé who'd abandoned her when times got tough, her manager who'd stolen from her.

But Ben—he might have broken her heart when she was a teenager, but he'd been young, too. And it was impossible not to admire and respect the man beside her. The man who fought when others would run. Who'd been wounded and still was determined to do his duty. Who reminded her that some men had truly good hearts.

If only she didn't love him so much.

"Stop poking me," Ben whispered to Rachel.

"Get. A. Clue," she whispered back, her gaze glued to the exchange of rings happening right in front of them.

Since he was in church, maybe the good Lord would have a direct view of what he had to put up with. Sisters. He loved them. He was glad he didn't visit home more often.

Okay, not exactly. He was going to miss them all a lot, especially Rachel. His medical leave was still active, but he was antsy to get back to base. Mainly because now it was going to be painful to stay around, thanks to the woman who perched on the pew on his other side. She sat silent and motionless, and yet every fiber of his being was aware of her every breath. And of her heartbeat, as if it were his own.

This is killing me. Watching Amy pledge her life to another was a great thing, but he never would have thought in a billion years that he'd be watching her get married and feeling bitter that he would never do the same. That he might want to.

Weren't weddings supposed to make women dream of their own wedding day? But not Cadence. She sat as still as stone, as stoic as a glacier. When the bride and groom kissed, sealing their vows, a sigh rose from the sanctuary. Even his chest caught tight, and he had a hard time breathing around the emotion lodged there.

He was happy for his sister. He was sad that his life would remain alone and empty. He cast a sideways look at Cadence. Lovely as always, with her hair back, revealing her delicate heart-shaped face and her roses-

and-cream skin. Her emotions shuttered like a window closed, covered and barred.

He never should have kissed her, he realized, rising to his feet as Amy and Heath turned, with Westin between them, officially man and wife. Applause broke out and rose petals showered the threesome as they headed down the aisle, beaming with happiness, blessed by the golden light from above.

· He sneaked another look out of the corner of his eye and saw that Cadence was swallowing hard, tears pooling like silver as she watched the threesome burst out into the sunshine, where more family members continued to cheer them. Cadence's bottom lip trembled, just once, a vulnerable gesture that made him wonder what she was thinking. What she was feeling. Her heart and her emotions were closed to him.

All he felt was utter devastation as he realized it was so over. He'd kissed her and the next time he'd seen her, she'd made it clear she wanted distance.

Her lips were rose-petal soft, and his

soul stirred with the wish to be the man to kiss her and love her for the rest of her life.

But some things were not meant to be. She might trust him as a friend, but she would not open her heart to him. And yet, was there a way? And why was he even thinking this? It was killing him, this agony thrumming like an open contusion between his ribs. He ought to let it go. Accept Cadence's distance. And let them both go on with their lives.

"Oh, Amy looks so happy, don't you think?" Rachel sniffled, swiping her eyes. "It's so g-good that she's h-hap-py."

"Are you crying, little sister?" He put his arm around her, turning toward his family instead of the other woman at his side. He didn't know what to do with her tears. He didn't know any longer what her dreams were.

"I'm just s-sappy. Don't mind me. I'm h-happy. R-really." She buried her face in his jacket and sobbed. "N-no one but us knows ho-ow hard she had it. And n-now…"

"A happy ending?" he finished.

She nodded, crying harder, this dear sister of his who wished on falling meteorite chunks and made s'mores cookies and put everybody in the world first before herself. He felt the hair on his nape prickle, and he knew the moment Cadence took a step away from him, walking to the far end of the pew and using the aisle there to escape.

Cadence. She'd had a hard road, too, and she deserved a happy ending.

And if not with me, Lord, he prayed, even though it was nearly killing him to imagine, *please find the right man for her. Because we both know it's not me.*

Sadness hit like an explosion, and he felt the light drain out of his soul. Leaving only shadows.

"I need cake," Rachel confessed as she wiped at her tears, shaking her head at herself. "Where did Cadence go?"

"Probably to congratulate the bride and groom, like everyone else."

"Thanks for letting me cry on you."

"I guess that's what big brothers are for."

"Yep." With a watery grin she slipped her arm through his. "What happened between you and Cadence? The last time I saw you two, you were kissing in the drive-way."

"Maybe she didn't like the kiss so much. Or me." That hurt, but Rachel might as well know it now. It seemed as if he walked in darkness and his feet were made of lead. How had he managed to let her so far into his heart?

"Oh, I don't know about that. She seemed pretty smitten with you."

"You read too many romance novels, sweetie."

"There's no such thing! There can never be too much romance in this world."

Not in his world. There was none, and there hadn't been any softness or love or comfort for so long, he hadn't realized how stark and bleak it was. Just work and duty and doing a job only those with iron will and steel nerves could do. But it was his life. It was what he had. And if he wanted Cadence… It's too bad, buddy. You have to go back.

The best thing to do was to avoid her. To keep his gaze from finding her in the crowd. To keep his soul from responding to hers so that there would be no more pain, no more devastation, no more loss.

Too late. The instant he followed Rachel through the doorway into the reception hall, his soul stirred at her presence. He turned to her like the earth to the sun, and his gaze found hers as if an invisible bond pulled them together. Even though he was doing his level best to tear them apart.

"There's Cadence." Rachel's hand pressed against his forearm, as if trying to will him into changing his mind about romance. "Take it from someone who's been waiting for love to come into my life for a long time, and it hasn't. If you love her, seize hold of it. Don't let it pass you by a second time. Why else did God bring Cadence back into our lives?"

"Coincidence?"

"Good try, big brother, but I don't think so." She pressed a kiss to his cheek, his sister who was sweet as pie, and left him standing alone as Cadence dipped her chin. She was in line to congratulate the bride and groom and slipped away, disappearing through the crowd.

Unfortunately for her, he was a soldier

trained for detail, and he didn't lose track of her. She was bypassing the beverage table and the cloth-draped tables full of candy and nut bowls and finger-food trays and past the caterers setting up for the buffet, heading for the side exit where she could slip away unnoticed.

She's leaving. The smart thing would be to let her go, because that's what she wanted. The trouble was, it wasn't what he wanted.

He realized he couldn't leave things like this between them. It would be no better than how it had been before when he'd run off to join the air force and left her behind to follow her dreams to Olympic gold. The trouble was that neither of them had ended up with the happiness they'd sacrificed to let the other find.

Is this in Your plan, Lord? Or am I trying to hang on to what I should let go of? He didn't know the answer. He only knew it felt as if his ribs were going to disintegrate from the agonizing pressure in his chest. From the wrenching emotional pain of facing his future without her.

He didn't know why he did it or what he

intended to do. He was simply marching
after her, weaving around small groups of
folks talking. Then dodging kids racing to
the refreshment tables and promising Ed
Brisbane and his buddies, who called for
him to join them, that he'd be back. It
seemed to take forever to wade through
the crowd to the side door, and he might
as well have been swimming against the
tide for all the progress he made.

Then finally he was pushing open the
door and emerging into the dazzling heat
and light, the grass lush and crisp beneath
his dress shoes as he yanked at the annoying monkey tie choking him at the throat.
He dragged in gulps of air, preparing to do
battle, preparing to face whatever it was he
had to. He had to know. He had to hear her
say the words, because if he went back to
Hurlburt and didn't know for sure if she
loved him, he wouldn't be able to stand it.
He'd never be able to put to rest this unbearable pain that was eating him up.

Feeling alone, he scanned the grounds.
No Cadence. Not on any of the benches.
Not seated beneath the shady trees. Where
had she gone? The blades of grass ruffled

in a whispering breeze. Leaves rustled overhead. The long low limbs of flowering cherries and the broad sturdy arms of the maples shaded him as he followed the light indentation of a woman's sandals, quite different from the boots of men he was used to tracking.

He followed her shoe prints to the far corner of the back lawn. To the left stretched the cemetery, markers solemn and flowers bright. To the right the land gave way to the wild sunflowers and crimson Indian paintbrush and thick bear grass dried to dark amber.

Cadence stood with wildflowers brushing her skirt, overlooking the wide Gallatin River, which sparkled in the bright day, rushing quiet and deep. She seemed lost in thought, watching the gleaming river. And with her back to him, she couldn't have heard him approach, although her spine stiffened and he watched tension creep into her shoulders.

She feels this, too, he realized. This synchronicity. This connection. Encouraged, he made his way through the dried grass that crunched beneath his uncomfortable shoes.

He yanked open the top buttons at his collar because his chest was tightening again and he needed every ounce of air he could drag into his lungs in order to get this out.

He had to know before he called his colonel and made the decision to come back early. He had to know there was no other possible future. No reason to stay in Montana a few more weeks while he could. Unless…

Unless. He stopped a few feet short of her. Jammed his hands into his pockets. Tried to figure out what to say. How to start. She didn't make it any easier. She didn't move. She didn't acknowledge him. She didn't give a hint as to whether she was being tortured by this, too—this not knowing, this fear of rejection, this overwhelming fear that maybe, just maybe, if they did it right, true love could have a second chance. That they could have a happy ending.

But where did he start?

The beach down below was busy. They were on the high end of the river. The bank rose a good ten yards higher on this side, giving way to a rock-and-clay beach below. Kids were taking advantage of the sizzling weather to escape into the cool river. Packs of kids on inner tubes floated by. A family in a motorboat. More kids roughhousing in the shallow waters by the shore.

"Once you're a lifeguard, you're always a lifeguard," he found himself saying. "I still can't just look at the river. I have to count heads and make sure everyone's accounted for."

"And be five steps ahead so you can stop disaster from happening." Cadence nodded, keeping her gaze on the swimmers and boaters below.

The high shrieks of kids at play peppered the air and emphasized the long silence that fell between them. Between the few feet separating them that felt as wide as the river.

I love you so much. He choked on the power of that single emotion. Not fear, not anger, nothing in his life had felt this much. Hurt this much. And yet when he laid his hand on her shoulder, ignoring the fact that she startled beneath his touch, the brightness in his soul returned. Radiance that made only one thing clear.

Heaven was giving him his answer.

He had everything to lose if he didn't tell her how he felt. If he did not risk everything right this minute. The future stood in the balance between them.

Since no words would come—he wasn't good with them anyway—he caught her face with both his hands, tipped it toward his and kissed her long and sure so she would know. So she would have to pull him close or push him away.

Chapter Fifteen

The first brush of Ben's kiss surprised her. She wasn't prepared for it. She hadn't imagined it. She'd expected him to kindly say goodbye. What else was there left to say between them? Shock filled her, and she couldn't react. She couldn't think, only feel as his kiss turned tender, a sweet, loving brush of his mouth to hers that seemed more like dream than reality.

But this was real. The agony in her heart. The sorrow in her soul. The breeze on her skin and the crisp sharp scent of dried grass and ripe wildflowers. The sharp rise and fall of kids screaming as they skidded down the fast river in their flotation devices.

Real, and no dream.

Ben was kissing her goodbye with all the tenderness of a wish come true. If this was the only tenderness she would know from this fine man he'd become, then it would have to be enough. She savored the strong feel of his heartbeat beneath her palms. The masculine scent of his after-shave. The luxury of his kiss.

Don't let this moment end, she prayed, for she was so grateful for it. For when the kiss ended and Ben moved away from her, he would be gone. All things ended, and she nearly cried out as he pulled his lips from hers. The love in her soul shone so brightly she could no longer see the sky or the river or even the man in front of her.

Or maybe that was the sun blurring in her tears. She swiped at her eyes, surprised her fingertips came away damp.

"You're crying." The caress of his baritone moved through her spirit, and she could feel his affection as his hand remained cradling her face, as if he could not bear to let her go.

Just as she clung to him, unable to make her hand release the handful of his jacket she'd only just realized she was squeezing. Self-conscious of her emotions, of the feelings that bubbled out of her no matter how hard she willed them down, she nodded her head, knowing she had to be honest.

In a way that she could keep her dignity and allow him to leave, she spoke only the truth. "I am crying. Amy has found happiness. Your leg will recover and you'll have what we've all been praying for. Good news all around. God is gracious."

"Yes, He is." Thoughtful, Ben did not move away. "What about you, Cadence? What about your happiness? What have you been praying for?"

"I've been praying for you—on your behalf," she corrected, the instant she realized her mistake. "I want only the best for you. Only the very best."

"That's what I want for you, too." He winced as if she'd struck him, and she didn't know why. "You have a lot here. Your work and your coaching."

"I do. It makes me happy." It was the truth. It was the only option she had. God had led her here, He'd been gracious to her despite so many mistakes in trusting people, and she was trying her best to let Ben go. To give him what made him happy.

But that's not entirely true, her conscience scolded her. When she looked into her heart she was afraid to trust that God might have brought her here to love this man, and she was too afraid. She was too afraid that as much as she'd wanted true love, it didn't often exist. She was afraid to put her trust in it one more time.

Ben had made no promises. No declarations. He'd spoken only of going back to his base. And if his kiss was like a dream of what true love should be...what about that? She didn't know. She only knew that it was safer to let him go.

His gaze turned fierce—not angry or threatening, but intense. And she felt the shock of it pierce her. As if he were trying to see the truth inside her.

"I know you love me. I can feel it here." His fist landed on his heart. "But what I want to know is if you love me enough? I've got almost three more years to go before I can retire. I'm in and there's nothing I can do about it. I have to go to Florida."

"I know you do." Pain wrenched through her. "Do you think this makes it easier to let you go, knowing this?"

"That's not what I'm asking, baby." The fierceness was gone and he was pulling her into his arms against his sun-warmed chest as dependable as steel, as safe as home, as real as forever.

"Then what are you asking me?"

Her eyes were wide with confusion. Didn't she know? His heart rent wide open, raw and more vulnerable than he'd ever let himself be before. It wasn't easy, this opening of himself, leaving the most vulnerable part of his spirit open and undefended. "I want to know if you might consider moving to Florida?"

Furrows dug into her forehead. "Are you asking me to?"

"I am asking everything, beautiful." He cleared his throat. *Help me find the words, Lord. Because I'm not good at this. I need Your guidance—*

An earsplitting scream rose from down below. They both automatically turned toward the sound. Where the wide, rolling river hit the rapids, a lone inner tube bobbed and raced past the pack of kids, who'd started shouting incoherently. One boy leaped off his tube and disappeared into the water. Then bobbed back, being swept away by the current.

There was only one thing to do. Ben hit the bank, skidding down the clay-and-rock cliffside, yanking off his tux jacket as he went. Wildflowers, scrub brush and saplings broke beneath his shoes as he kept his eye on the spot where he'd first seen the lone inner tube. He was hardly aware of anything except the crush of crumbling earth behind him. Cadence. She was coming, too.

"You go after the kid in the current," he ordered her, but there was no need. She was already cutting to his right, downriver, her shoes gone, and they were moving as a team.

There was no more need for words, he knew. They leaped into the river, running into the water, pushing into the deeper water until the current caught them.

Ben scissor kicked hard into the fierce river, ignoring the chaos around him, figuring out where the submerged kid might be. He hadn't come up—anything could have happened. But the current was strong, and it was shallower here where huge boulders beneath the surface made a dangerous ripple in the current.

He dived, eyes open, searching the rocky riverbed for anything unusual. Summer trout as big as his arm skidded out of his way and he spied a tennis shoe. The teenager was crushed against a granite outcropping, pinned in place by the current's undertow. His eyes were wild with panic.

Ben planted his feet, grabbed the kid firmly around the wrist, twisted and pulled. Piece of cake. The boy spun away from the boulder and into his arms. Before the boy's panic could take control, Ben calmly wrapped him in a cross-chest carry and kicked off from the river's floor.

Silt kicked up to cloud the water around them as they bobbed to the surface.

A hysterical woman was making her way into the dangerous current. The kid's mom.

Ben shouted at her, "He's fine, I've got him. Go back!"

Before the woman could get herself into

trouble, too, there was Cadence, taking her by the forearm and talking calmly to her. They waited as he hauled the boy in, and the teenager was already struggling, but no longer from panic.

"Hey, let me go!" He coughed, fighting, indignant.

Ben let the kid take over. He wasn't hurt, just scared. And embarrassed in front of his friends.

"Where is your life jacket, young man?" his mother demanded in a voice filled with relief and outrage at the same time. "And thank these fine people for helping you."

"Uh…thanks."

"No problem," Ben assured them both, watching the mother grab her son by the ear and haul him toward the picnic area.

A glance downstream told him Cadence had been successful at reuniting the boy with his tube, and he was floating away with his friends, distant on the swift current. He and Cadence made quite a team. She was dripping wet, her silk dress soaked and probably ruined by the river water, but she didn't look troubled by it.

His soul filled with light, more blinding than the sun, as endless as eternity.

She swiped a strand of hair out of her face. "What were you saying—something like once a lifeguard, always a lifeguard?"

"Yeah. Or maybe it's just us."

"We're both out to save the world in our different ways." She shrugged. "Well, I'm not saving the world."

"It's how you live your life every day, helping people. Teaching kids to swim so they won't drown some day."

Her smile was pure radiance. "Then you understand."

His entire being ached with love for her. He took her by the hand while the river rushed by and the picnickers went back to their picnics and kids splashed in the shallow water. He led her toward the bank where wildflowers carpeted their path.

It felt right, holding her hand, walking at her side where he wanted to be for the rest of his life. She was his home, his everything. "I was hoping you'd like to teach kids to swim and dive in Florida. If you'd consider giving up everything here to marry me? To be my wife?"

There, he'd said it. The toughest task he'd ever had put in front of him, and he trembled with the importance of it. Everything he'd ever wanted rested on what this incredible, awesome woman would say next. He'd faced ambushes, night fighting, freeing soldiers held prisoner, but he'd never been so afraid and so certain of what he wanted.

"You want me to marry you?" She stared up at him as if afraid to believe. "You want me to marry you," she repeated as if she couldn't believe what he'd said.

The anxiety tight in his chest disappeared, because he felt her answer in his soul. True love was strong enough to build a future on. He knew this now, for he saw their future happy and loving stretch out before him—a fulfilling marriage, a happy home and kids. A little girl and a little boy.

Nice. And he'd retire in a few years, and they'd come home here, to Montana. But until then, he'd do what he could for his country. And then give everything to his family.

She came into his arms like a dream. She felt the choice before her—to trust him wholly, this man heaven kept bringing into her life, or to turn away everything that God was offering her.

"Yes, I'll marry you." She laid her hand on his jaw, this wonderful hero of her very own. This man who filled her soul. Who was her life.

Thank You, Lord, she prayed, aware of this great blessing heaven was giving her. "I've always wanted a September wedding."

Epilogue

Two weeks later

Sunlight glinted through the high windows in the rafters and into Cadence's eyes. She wanted to blame her tears on the sun, and not the sentimental feelings rising from her heart. Because if she admitted her feelings, on this last day of coaching, then she would break down in endless tears.

As sad as this door closing in her life was, a wonderful new one was opening. Her wedding was tomorrow. A new life was beginning. First with a honeymoon cruise to Alaska and then the long-distance move to Florida. So much change, but it was exciting, too.

Opening her heart to Ben's love had been worth the risk.

"I'm gonna, like, really miss you." Ashley climbed out of the diving pool, water sluicing off her, from the last dive of her lesson. "I'm never gonna find another coach like you. Dad says he's gonna put in for a transfer. So maybe I can still keep training with you."

"That would be great, Ashley. You have my e-mail address, right? So we can keep in contact no matter what. I want to know how you progress with that armstand forward somersault. Promise?"

"Like, I totally promise!" Ashley grabbed her towel from the bench and draped it over her shoulders. From her pack, slumped on the bench, she withdrew a small wrapped box. "A wedding gift. Kinda early, but it's little, so I didn't want it to get lost with all the others you're probably gonna get. Don't open it, cuz I'll be embarrassed." Ashley gave a long sigh and blinked hard, but the tears came anyway. "Like, I don't wanna say goodbye."

"I know. I'll be coming home to visit. I

promise I'll come here and we can work on your dives."

"Really? That's so cool! Thanks, Cadence!" Relieved that this wasn't a final goodbye, Ashley scampered off to the locker rooms, leaving her alone.

Her last day. She'd had some great times in this pool. It was her first real job, aside from picking berries in the field, which she'd got when she was fifteen.

She'd trained here as a girl filled with impossible dreams. She'd come back when most of those dreams had shattered. And rebuilt her life…and she'd learned to dream again.

Only, this time she knew her dreams of happily ever after would not fail. She knew, because of Ben. There was no man more dependable, more true. And he was hers.

Ben. She felt him like a change in the air. He was here. Her soul stirred and she turned toward him, always to him, the man she loved more than her life. Her soul mate.

Her one true love.

He came to her with open arms and

hauled her against his strong chest. His kiss was a tender promise. His joy was hers.

"I'm on my way out to the airport, to pick up Jake." His closest buddy on his squad and his best man at their wedding. "But I wanted to stop by here first. I had to see you one more time."

"I thought we were having dinner in, what, three hours?"

"Yeah, but I missed you." He kissed her again. "I'll pick up Jake, get him settled and then I'll be out to pick you up."

It had been Ben's idea for them to spend the evening before their wedding together. He'd made reservations at an exclusive restaurant at a Bozeman resort that served only the finest meals. A five-course intimate dinner awaited them, with dazzling views of the river and the incredible mountains. Hours spent alone, just the two of them, planning, talking, cuddling.

"Will your friend be all right alone?"

"Jake's an independent guy. He'll be fine. Besides, I sweet-talked Rachel into cooking dinner for him at the house. She promised to feed him, keep him company and hand over the remote control." He pulled back enough to study her face as he asked, "Are you too sad about leaving here? Am I asking you to give up too much?"

"No. I'm sad, but I can work in Florida, too. And Ben, look at what I'm getting. You."

Her dear, strong, wonderful Ben. To have and to hold. To love and to cherish. For all the days of her life. "I can't wait until tomorrow. Our wedding day. The start of our life together."

"And it will be happy." And like a promise meant to be kept, he kissed her long and sweetly.

* * * * *

Be sure to check out Jillian Hart's next inspirational romance, BLESSED VOWS, available December 2005.

Dear Reader,

The McKaslin family story continues when brother Ben returns from active duty in the Middle East. He'd been injured in combat and he's not sure if his injuries will heal enough for him to return to the career he loves and feels called to do. As courageous as he's been as a pararescueman defending our country, he finds real peril returning to his hometown in Montana—the danger of opening his heart to his high school sweetheart, Cadence. God is always gracious and gives him a little help along the way.

Thank you for choosing *Heaven's Touch*. I hope you enjoy Ben's story as much as I've enjoyed writing it.

I wish you joy and the sweetest of blessings.

Jillian Hart